Alaska Emergency Docs

Welcome to Anchorage Memorial Hospital, where the busy medics of the ER save lives every day, but healing their own hearts is another matter entirely.

It might be cold outside, but inside things are heating up with the arrival of Dr. Georgia Sumter. A former resident of the town, she fled three years ago after a disastrous breakup with local hot doc Eli Jacobsen. Can they work together in harmony, or will history get the better of them? One thing's for certain—when these two are reunited, sparks are sure to fly!

Meanwhile, the ER's grapevine is buzzing with the news of Dr. Jessie Davis's surprise pregnancy. Rumor has it that the good doctor's best friend, nurse William Harris, is the father! Will the transition from pals to parents be smooth sailing, or will that pesky attraction they discovered one night change their lives completely...?

Find out what happens in the exciting
Alaska Emergency Docs duet!

Eli and Georgia's story
Reunion with the ER Doctor by Tina Beckett

William and Jessie's story
One-Night Baby with Her Best Friend by Juliette Hyland

Available now!

Dear Reader,

I don't know about you, but I have some little quirks... okay, irrational fears that are carried over from my childhood. I can't bring myself to drink the last inch or so of milk left in the container. Or orange juice or tea or any kind of beverage. And if it's close to the expiration date, it's even worse.

Georgia Sumter has a phobia too, but it's much bigger than something as inconsequential as drinking the remainder of milk. She has a fear of commitment, and it shows up in a big way when Eli Jacobsen asks her to marry him. It causes her to run.

Thank you for joining Eli and Georgia as they go on a journey of overcoming fears and facing some hard truths. And maybe they'll find a way through those fears and find their way back to each other. I hope you love reading their story as much as I loved writing it.

Love,

Tina Beckett

REUNION WITH THE ER DOCTOR

TINA BECKETT

MEDICAL ROMANCE

MEDICAL ROMANCE

Recycling programs for this product may not exist in your area.

ISBN-13: 978-1-335-94250-0

Reunion with the ER Doctor

Harlequin Enterprises ULC
22 Adelaide St. West, 41st Floor
Toronto, Ontario M5H 4E3, Canada
www.Harlequin.com

Printed in U.S.A.

Three-time Golden Heart® Award finalist **Tina Beckett** learned to pack her suitcases almost before she learned to read. Born to a military family, she has lived in the United States, Puerto Rico, Portugal and Brazil. In addition to traveling, Tina loves to cuddle with her pug, Alex; spend time with her family; and hit the trails on her horse. Learn more about Tina from her website or friend her on Facebook.

Books by Tina Beckett

Harlequin Medical Romance

Buenos Aires Docs

ER Doc's Miracle Triplets

California Nurses

The Nurse's One-Night Baby

One Night with the Sicilian Surgeon
From Wedding Guest to Bride?
A Family Made in Paradise
The Vet, the Pup and the Paramedic
The Surgeon She Could Never Forget
Resisting the Brooding Heart Surgeon
A Daddy for the Midwife's Twins?
Tempting the Off-Limits Nurse

Visit the Author Profile page
at Harlequin.com for more titles.

As always to my family. I love you!

PROLOGUE

HER GAZE FOLLOWED the bright pink piggy bank as it sailed through the air and then crashed to the ground with a shattering sound that seemed to go on forever. Something hit her hand, causing her to jerk in pain as she stared at all the silver coins and sharp pieces of glass that lay all around her. Then she started crying, unable to stop, even though she knew it would only make things worse.

"Georgia, do not move." Her mom's shaky voice reached her, even as her daddy stood over her, looking bigger and scarier than he ever had before.

Georgia, still in her nightgown—her feet bare, started to take a step back to get away from him, except her mother reached her first and scooted in front of her, staring up at the man in front of her.

"Get out. Get out now." The words were

said with a soft hiss that made Georgia shiver, stopping her tears in an instant.

She had never heard her mom speak to her dad like that. Ever. Normally she was saying she was sorry to him over and over for things that Georgia didn't understand. But not today.

She leaned to peer around her mom in an effort to see her father's reaction, and it was strange. He no longer seemed mad. Instead he looked as if didn't understand something before he seemed to notice Georgia. His arm came forward, beckoning her over to him. Her mother smacked his hand away, pulling her phone out and pushing some buttons.

Evidently that meant something to her father because he backed up a step, the anger coming back to his face. "You'll be begging me to come back. You can't make it on your own."

There was a long silence, then her mom, phone still in her hand, seemed to grow taller right in front of Georgia's eyes. "You just watch me, Gavin."

Her dad threw his can of beer at the wall, and it made an ugly *thunk* as it fell, its contents spilling all over their only rug. Then he turned around and jerked the front door open and stomped out, not bothering to close it behind him. Snow began blowing into the room, turning it icy in an instant. Then he disappeared into the night.

Her mom rushed over and slammed the door shut, locking it and leaning against it for a second. Georgia wasn't the only one crying—her mom was too. "A-Are you okay, baby?"

She nodded. "But my new bank… Santa brought it for me."

"We'll get you another one. We'll…" She stopped, and her eyes went to a spot on the floor. "You're bleeding."

Georgia looked down and saw that something red was dripping from her hand. Startled by the dark color, she held it up and stared at it. A scary feeling went through her. "Mama, I think I'm hurt."

Her mom quickly grabbed a blanket from the nearby sofa and threw it over the floor in front of Georgia. As she walked across it, the pieces of the bank made a dull crunching sound under her feet. Then she picked up Georgia and carried her to a clean spot on the plank flooring. Looking at her hand, her mom's eyes closed for a second. Then she went into action, grabbing some tissues and the tape that she'd used to wrap Christmas presents before covering the place on Georgia's hand. It hurt. "Let me get your coat."

"But my bank…"

"We'll take care of that later. Right now we need to get your wrist looked at."

Within minutes, they were both bundled in coats and boots and they were driving through the snow. Georgia wondered if her dad would be back when they got home.

She didn't think so. For some reason she didn't think he'd ever be home again.

CHAPTER ONE

GEORGIA SUMTER TOUCHED the scar on her left wrist as she walked through the doors of Anchorage Memorial Hospital. It looked exactly the same as it had when she'd left three years ago. It was funny how some things never changed, while other things changed forever.

Kind of like her childhood home, which was long gone. Her mom had been awarded the house in the divorce, but they hadn't stayed there. She'd sold it almost immediately, moving Georgia into a smaller one-bedroom home that, although cramped, had felt safe in a way that their other house hadn't. Only as she'd gotten older had she understood why that was.

Her pink piggy bank had been replaced with a big white rabbit bank. By the time she'd been eighteen, it had been stuffed to the gills with both coins and bills, although she'd never broken it open to get at the money, since the sound of anything shattering still had the ability to make her nerves take a giant leap, along with her heart rate.

She shook away the thoughts. The decision to return to Anchorage Memorial hadn't been an easy one. Not after all that had happened here. But taking a leave of absence from the hospital and running back to her hometown on Kodiak Island hadn't been the best idea either. She'd thought being near her mom would help her feel cocooned and allow healing to begin. And it had—in the beginning. But her mom's almost daily assurances that she'd done the right thing had eventually become like a funeral dirge, dark and repetitive and…unbearable. The cocoon had transformed into something claustrophobic. As had the small clinic where she'd opted to work once she'd made the decision to resign from Anchorage Memorial. There'd been no worries about seeing her dad. He no longer lived in the town. In fact, she had no idea where he was anymore, and she was okay with it staying that way.

A familiar face crossed the hallway, glancing her way before backtracking and then staring at her as if he thought he was seeing things. Finally his head cocked sideways. "Georgia?"

Her hair was about twelve inches shorter than it had been three years ago, now hanging just past her shoulders in choppy layers, and her bleached locks had been allowed to return to their natural dark brown waves. She could understand why he was taken aback. That plus the fact that she'd once told him she'd never return to the hospital that she'd loved so much.

"It's me. Just a little older and hopefully wiser than the last time you saw me."

William Harris turned and came toward her. "I had no idea you were in town. Last I heard from you, you were still on Kodiak."

Her childhood friend, who'd been with her through thick and thin, had grown up on the same Alaskan island as she had, but he had left when he'd been eighteen. They'd kept in touch all these years, though, and had worked together at Anchorage Memorial until she'd made the agonizing decision to leave.

But she'd missed her life here. So very much. So much so that she was willing to risk seeing…

No. Don't think about that.

She reached into her pocket to find her

charm and frowned when she realized she'd left her necklace in the car. She'd taken it off that morning to shower, and in her hurry to make it to the hospital on time, she'd tossed it into the glove compartment. Which was where it still was.

"I decided to come back. I missed the hospital—" she smiled at him "—and my friends. And enough time has passed that I think I'm up for it. Besides, Eli is married now, so it should be just—"

He frowned. "Hell, Georgia, why didn't you let me know you were thinking of coming back?"

His response stopped her flat. "I thought you'd be happy to see me."

He gripped her hand for a second and squeezed before letting go. "Of course I am. It's just that Eli isn't..."

Had her ex left the area? Even though that would be an even better scenario—letting her go back to life before she'd met him—something in her stomach sloshed at the thought of never seeing him again.

Isn't that what you'd hoped by leaving here three years ago?

Yes. She'd intended to put him in her past as firmly as she'd put her dad in the past. Except her reasons for doing so had been completely different. Eli had been nothing but supportive. He'd just wanted more than she could give.

"Did he move away?"

"No." William's voice came back, and he looked in her face. "But he's not married anymore either. He and Lainey got divorced a little over a year ago."

Her heart shot straight into her throat. Not married? "Why didn't you tell me?"

"I didn't think you were coming back and didn't figure you'd want to be kept up to date with everything Eli's been up to, considering how you guys left things. Besides, you kept saying that things on Kodiak were going great."

That's what she got for lying. Her hand went into her pocket again. She normally kept the butterfly with her as a reminder to always be free. She fiddled with it whenever she was stressed. And right now definitely fit that bill.

"I know. And of course I didn't want you to tell me everything. It's my fault for not saying anything about coming back. I just happened to see an ad for the ER position on a job board as I was looking for somewhere new to go. HR let me know almost immediately that they wanted me back, so I was busy trying to get things situated before leaving Kodiak General." She shrugged. "I thought I'd surprise you."

"Consider me surprised. In a good way." A smile accompanied the words. "I knew we were getting someone else. I just didn't bother to look to see if there was a name attached. I was just hoping it wasn't going to be another Dr. Mueller."

"Dr. Mueller?" That name didn't ring a bell.

William's brows went up. "Yep. Ronny Mueller. He actually took your place when your decision not to come back was finalized. And let's just say things haven't been the same since then. I wouldn't be surprised if he was part of the reason why Dr. Hawthorne left the ER."

"Oh! That's too bad. I really liked Becky."

Becky Hawthorne had been one of her good friends at Anchorage Memorial. Georgia had been looking forward to working with her again. In fact, Becky had tried to convince her not to leave…to give it some time. She didn't realize the open position had been the result of Becky leaving. She got an itchy feeling that her reasons for coming back were beginning to unravel.

"We all did. But she decided to go work at one of the smaller neighboring clinics. So she's still around." He shrugged. "Well, I'm glad you're back. More than you know. Are you working today?"

"No, I'm just going to HR to do some paperwork. I think I officially start tomorrow. I guess they'll tell me when I get there. Speaking of which, I'd better go before I'm late."

He smiled. "Would that really be something new?"

She swatted his arm. "I'm trying to turn over a new leaf."

"I'll believe it when I see it. Let's get together for lunch sometime, okay?"

She grinned back at him, trying not to think about Eli or what she was going to say to him when she eventually ran into him. "You've got it. And I promise I'll be on time."

He made a sound in the back of his throat. William was a hunk, and she was surprised he hadn't found someone by now.

But then again, neither had she. Nor did she want to. Her mom had spun enough cautionary tales to last a lifetime. Georgia had been willing to date, since getting out of those types of relationships were a lot less messy than a divorce. She'd proven that when she'd left Anchorage three years ago. But marriage? Her mom had had a heck of a time getting free of her husband. What Georgia hadn't known as a child was that her dad had actually fought for custody of her and had almost won, spinning tales of neglect and abuse. Which was so laughable, since it had been the other way around.

So yeah. Marriage and children? They didn't spell freedom in Georgia's book.

"Okay," William said. "Let me know when you get your schedule. I'd better get back to the floor too."

He retraced his steps and headed toward the emergency department, while Georgia made her way to the elevator.

God, Eli wasn't married anymore? That was one of the reasons she'd been tempted to take the job. She knew them both well enough to know that neither she nor Eli would ever cheat on someone, so she'd figured she'd be safe. They both would. The fact that Eli had married someone they'd both known from the hospital a little over a year after they'd parted had been soul wrenching, especially since Georgia had not so much as dated in all that time. But it also confirmed that she'd been right to walk away.

And now?

As soon as she got back to her car, she was going to dig that charm out of the glove box and put the talisman back around her neck. Then she'd make sure she had it with her wherever she went.

Eli stripped off his surgical gloves and tossed them into the bin before pushing through the double doors that led out of the operating room. The surgery to implant a biventricular pacemaker had been tricky, and he'd almost lost the patient twice before he'd even cracked open her chest. In the later stage of heart failure due to arrhythmias, her heart rate had been dangerously low. But the new pacemaker was geared to coordinate the rhythm between the chambers and would hopefully give the fifty-year-old a chance for a better quality of life. He'd combined it with an implantable defibrillator in case her heart decided to arrest again.

He still wasn't sure what the final outcome would be, but what he did know was that without surgery, his patient hadn't had a chance. She probably would have been dead in a matter of weeks, if not days. Right now, her heart was still weak, but it was at least beating in sync and at a better rate. Given time, the organ might even be able to regain some strength. Only time would tell.

He was due to have lunch with his good friend Steve Davis, who'd retired from his family practice several years ago. If not for Steve, Eli might not have been doing what he loved most in life. Eli's job had lasted longer than either of his romantic relationships, in fact. And he didn't see that changing anytime soon. Steve had been best man at his wedding, and although his friend had smiled and said all the right things, Eli had been able to tell he hadn't been sure about how well matched he and Lainey were. And he'd been right. Would he have had the same attitude if his bride had been Georgia?

No use even thinking along those lines, because Georgia had made it very clear that she didn't want that kind of relationship. He just wasn't sure why she'd waited so long to make that fact crystal clear. She could have saved them both a lot of heartache if she had. If he'd thought about it, though, the signs had all been there: Her quick, vague answers whenever he'd asked her about her childhood or her parents. The fact that she'd rarely talked about plans for the future, saying she preferred to live in the moment, because you never knew what life would throw at you. And he'd made a mistake by not gradually introducing the idea of marriage and feeling her out before just jumping in with a proposal. That had been an impulse decision, although he'd had the ring for months.

Lainey Grant had been right there to offer him a shoulder to cry on. He and Georgia had both worked with the hospital's pediatrician. But she'd listened and gone to the bar with him, being his designated driver when he'd gotten roaring drunk the night after Georgia had said the fateful words, *I'm so sorry, Eli. I just don't want to get married. Not to you. Not to anyone. It's not you. It's me.* And while Georgia hadn't officially broken things off, her message had been clear. As had her sudden decision to take a leave of absence.

And Lainey… Well, she'd seemed to be everything that Georgia was not. She'd been an open book when it came to her past. And she'd seemed to have the same interests and hopes for the future that he did. And eight months later, things had just kind of spiraled out of control when they'd slept together. Suddenly they'd been planning a wedding with a speed that had made his head spin. God, what a mess he'd made of that too. Maybe Georgia was right about marriage being a crock.

He took the elevator down to the ground floor, walking past a set of offices. His glance swung that way when he detected movement through the large glass panels next to the door. He stopped in his tracks, baffled... wondered if his earlier thoughts had suddenly summoned an apparition. An apparition he had no desire to see.

And it definitely wasn't Lainey.

His jaw hardened when he realized it was no apparition. The person was very real—a blast from the past. In the flesh.

What in the hell is she doing here?

His glance went back to the stenciled label on the door.

Human Resources.

There was no way. Life would not be that unkind. Would it?

The door opened with a swish, but her head was still cranked sideways, looking at someone inside the room. "Thanks. I'll stop in for my lanyard on my way in tomorrow, okay?"

"Lanyard?" He hadn't realized he'd growled the word aloud until she turned his way, suddenly white-knuckling the door as if she needed it for support.

"Eli."

Unlike him, there was no question mark behind the whispered word. She knew exactly who he was. The only question was, why was she back?

"Yes, it's me, Georgia. Surely you haven't forgotten?"

She let go of the door, and he watched as it swung silently back into place, but he could see Adrienne, the director of the department, staring at them with what looked like dismay.

Well, she wasn't the only one.

"No, well, um…" Her teeth came down on her lip in a way that was all too familiar to him. She'd done it that last day they'd been together. Right after he'd asked her to marry him.

He decided to interrupt her before she said something he didn't want to hear. Although he couldn't think of anything he *did* want to hear. Not from her.

"Why are you here?" If the words sounded a little harsh, even to his own ears, he didn't try to backtrack or soften them. Realizing Adrienne was still looking at them, he motioned to the corridor across from them which contained nothing but janitorial closets and supplies. Once there he stopped again, making sure they were no longer in the line of sight of anyone from HR.

She glanced up at him, her chin jutting out. "I'm, um, taking Becky Hawthorne's place. She…er, left."

Did she even realize how that sounded? "That seems to be a common trait among ER doctors at Anchorage Memorial." His eyes speared hers. "Leaving, I mean."

She shook her head. "I know what you meant, and it wasn't very nice. I'm sure Becky had her reasons."

"I'm not a very nice guy. Not anymore. And I'm sure she did. It still doesn't completely answer my question. *Why* are you here?" This time he made sure to stress the first word in that phrase.

"Because I missed the hospital. Missed my friends here in Anchorage."

Missed the hospital and her friends, but not him. That omission was glaring. But then again, he hadn't expected her to declare her undying love for him.

"So you're headed back to our emergency room."

She took a step closer. "Is that so bad? We've both moved on with our lives, Eli.

Surely we can work in the same hospital, if not in the same department."

They could. But it didn't mean he had to be happy about it. "So if we were in the same department, you wouldn't have applied for the job?"

She looked at his face for a long time. "Probably not."

Then maybe he should've been sorry that she wasn't a heart doctor because this moment wouldn't have been happening if that were the case. "I'm sure we can avoid crossing each other's paths if we try hard enough."

Her teeth came down on that soft lower lip again before she released it, sending a spike to his gut.

"Just for the record, Eli, I'm sorry. I thought you were married, or I never would have—"

One of the nurses he recognized from the ER came skidding around the corner before stopping in front of them. "Adrienne told me she thought you went this way." The man threw a glance Eli's way before looking back at Georgia. "Sorry. Am I interrupting something?"

Oh, now he remembered who the nurse was. He was Georgia's childhood friend, William.

"It's fine." Georgia tilted her head. "Is something wrong?"

"I'm not sure. Can you come with me to talk to a patient? Dr. Mueller saw her, but there's just something…"

"Of course I can." The relief in her voice would have been comical, except there was nothing funny about Georgia suddenly showing up at the hospital. "I'll see you later, Eli."

Before he could say he hoped not, the pair turned and hurried away, William explaining something about whatever patient it was before they disappeared from sight.

Eli muttered a few choice words under his breath before giving up and heading toward his appointment with Steve.

Georgia was back. And he had no idea what to think about that, much less what his attitude was going to be. But he'd better figure it out and soon. Before they ran into each other again. Because despite his earlier words, he was sure it was bound to happen. And when it did, he wanted to be ready.

"Like I was saying, she complained of her heart suddenly racing without warning and Mueller completely blew her off. Offered to prescribe her antianxiety meds without running any testing other than the standard EKG."

"What makes you think it's something more?"

William shrugged. "Maybe because she didn't look relieved. If anything, it seemed like it was exactly what she'd expected him to say. Like she'd heard it before. Or maybe it's just because it's not the first time I've seen Mueller dismiss a patient's concerns, and one time it…well, it didn't end well for the patient."

"Okay. Which room is she in?"

"Three. Hopefully she's still there."

When they swung the door open, though, there was only a nurse in there wiping down the exam table. "Where's Molly Breckin?"

"Who?"

"The patient who was just in this room."

"She just left. Before Dr. Mueller could even come back with the paperwork."

"Damn."

The nurse looked closer at William before her face cleared. "You might still be able to catch her before she makes it to the parking lot. And by the way, I agree with you."

He didn't stop to ask what she meant, just glanced at Georgia. "Come on."

They hurried to the nearest exit, and William said, "There she is."

Georgia saw a slim young woman walking down the sidewalk, her head bowed and shoulders slumped—an air of defeat that was hard to miss. They pushed through the doors and called out to her.

"Ms. Breckin, could you wait for a minute?"

The slight form stiffened before turning toward them. "I've already tried antianxiety meds, and they did no good. Besides, it happens at times when I'm not stressed, like when I'm sitting down or reading. It's even woken me up from a sound sleep."

Georgia reached a hand toward her. "Why don't you come back inside, and we'll talk some more."

"Who are you?"

"I'm Dr. Sumter."

Molly sighed. "It won't do any good. The other doctor already did an EKG, just like the other doctors I've seen. And they never see anything because it's not happening when the machine is on."

"But…"

The other woman's head jerked from side to side. "No. I'm done with doctors. So far whatever it is hasn't killed me, so how dangerous can it be?"

Georgia's chest ached. It could be really dangerous, depending on what was causing the arrhythmia. She'd seen a seemingly healthy teenager drop dead from a cardiac problem that had gone undiagnosed. Most people never saw it coming. "Won't you reconsider? There might be—"

"No."

She looked at the woman for a minute, then took a piece of paper from a pad in her purse and wrote her name and cell-phone number on it. "If you change your mind, please give me a call. It doesn't matter when. If I happen to be with a patient, I'll call you back as soon as I'm done."

Molly's eyes widened, and she hesitated before reaching her hand out for the paper. "Okay." Then she gave a slight smile that made Georgia's heart ache even more. "You're the first doctor who's acted like they believed me. Thank you."

And before she or William could say anything else, the woman turned and continued down the sidewalk without looking back.

Georgia reached over and squeezed William's hand. "You did what you could."

"Then why doesn't it feel like enough?"

She couldn't answer that question because Georgia had asked herself that same thing over and over. There were those patients who you felt you'd failed. Like you could have given more to...done more for. And yet when you looked back, you were never quite sure what you could have done to make the conclusion any more satisfying.

Kind of like how things had ended with Eli. It had been anything but satisfying. And yet whenever she posed the question to herself, she couldn't think of anything she would have done differently. Because when it came down to it, she'd needed to leave. Not just for herself, but to save Eli a whole lot of heartache as well.

CHAPTER TWO

ELI WAS WORKING on paperwork the next evening when a knock came at his door. Without looking up, he said, "Come in."

He glanced up to see the one person he hadn't expected. At least not so quickly. And he certainly hadn't expected her to seek him out. "I thought we agreed to avoid each other."

"I know, and I'm sorry, but…" She didn't open the door all the way, instead simply asking, "Do you have a minute?"

Setting his pen down, he sighed. "You might as well come in."

It wasn't a very cordial invitation, but it was the only one he had right now. He still hadn't gotten over the shock of seeing her earlier.

Georgia came in and closed the door behind herself before perching in a chair in front of the desk. "I have kind of an odd question."

He couldn't imagine anything coming from her that wasn't "odd" at this point. "Okay."

"It's about a patient."

About a thousand muscles in his body relaxed. At least she didn't want to talk about anything personal. Although why did that surprise him? Did he really expect her to come in and ask to take up where they'd left off? Or try to explain things from three years earlier?

According to the dream he'd had last night that was exactly what had transpired, and like an idiot, his dream self had wrapped her in his arms and kissed her before taking things much further. He'd woken up in a cold sweat, and even at the memory, his muscles were now bunching up all over again.

He shook off the thoughts and looked at her. "Which patient is that?" A thought came to him. "The one from yesterday, when William came to get you?"

She nodded. "She's not exactly my patient—she's Dr. Mueller's."

Eli gave an audible groan. "Dr. Mueller is pretty territorial about his patients. I've tangled with him a couple of times, and it's never been a whole lot of fun."

"And if a patient's life is on the line, would you tangle with him again?"

"Hell, Georgia, he's only here because of you."

She blinked, looking stricken all of a sudden. "What?"

He'd made it sound like she was at fault for that. And maybe part of it was that he blamed her for taking off the way she had three years ago. "I mean, he took your place."

"I had no control over that."

No. She hadn't. But she'd had control over what she'd done before that. When she'd decided to leave the hospital. And him. But it wouldn't help anyone to keep reliving what had happened back then. "I realize that. What's the problem? I can't guarantee I can help, though, unless Mueller brings me in on the case."

"Well…" This time her eyes wouldn't quite meet his. "She's not exactly at the hospital anymore."

Had the patient died? "Meaning what?"

"She left AMA."

Against medical advice. Doctors universally hated it when that happened. "I take it she was a cardiac patient?"

"No. At least not officially. Because he didn't believe her."

"Who didn't?"

She frowned at him as if he were dense. "Mueller didn't."

Eli had heard murmurs about Mueller— that he tended to coast along in the ER and avoided the more complex cases if he could help it. "Maybe you'd better explain exactly what is bothering you."

The fact that William had come to get her meant that it had bothered the nurse too. Enough to bypass the doctor assigned to the case, which was a very big deal at Anchorage Memorial. And since Georgia had come to see him, it meant she agreed with William.

"I didn't examine her, but I did read her file." She went on to tell him about a young female patient who'd come in complaining about periodic episodes of racing heartbeats. That in and of itself wasn't cause for alarm, especially given the age of the patient. Until he heard that she'd consulted several doctors and they'd all diagnosed her with anxiety.

That sent up an alarm, especially since, according to Georgia, the patient had tried the meds they'd offered and they hadn't helped.

"What tests were run?"

"At other hospitals? I have no idea. But here at ours, she got a fifteen-second EKG, which was declared unremarkable."

Her face showed her thoughts about that.

But then again, she'd never been good at hiding her emotions, whether she was happy or sad or at the heights of ecstasy. And when she was at those heights…

Irritation spiked through him, and he forced his brain back to what she'd said about the patient.

EKGs certainly had their place, but for idiopathic arrhythmias they were close to useless since if the heart wasn't out of rhythm at that specific moment, it could be dismissed, much like Mueller had done with the patient. Eli certainly wouldn't have stopped at an "unremarkable" tracing. "Did she tell Mueller that she'd seen other doctors?"

Her nose squinched in a way he remembered all too well. It indicated frustration. Or embarrassment. "I'm not sure, but she told William and me that she had."

"If she left AMA, how did she tell you that?"

"William and I kind of chased her into the parking lot."

"You kind of chased her…" Hell, if that didn't sound like something Georgia would do. For some reason the picture of her and William running after some patient and then grilling her about her condition struck him as humorous, and he couldn't hold back a chuckle.

"What's so funny?"

"Oh, certainly not the patient's story. But the fact that you charged after her and...what? Tried to get her to come back inside? Have you even officially started your job yet?"

"Well...yes to the first question and no to the second. I start tomorrow."

"Then you know that she would have been bounced right back to Mueller."

"Not if I could have reached you before he found out about it."

Wow, so she would have asked *him* to bypass Mueller? That could have gone badly in so many ways. For both Georgia and himself. But he couldn't blame her. She was nothing if not a tireless advocate for her patients. So it shouldn't have surprised him that she would have risked the wrath of a colleague for a patient that wasn't even hers. It was one of the things he'd loved about her.

Loved. Past tense.

As if realizing the possible outcome, she shook her head. "I'm sorry. I shouldn't have even come here or said anything."

Yes, she should have. Because if she had succeeded in getting the patient back inside and had brought her up to the fourth floor, he would have undoubtedly taken a closer look at her. He'd already had it out with Mueller about one patient. The other doctor had ultimately backed down when it had turned out that Eli had been right about the patient needing a heart cath. But if the patient hadn't even been referred to a cardiac doctor? He was pretty sure Mueller would have lodged a complaint against both Georgia and himself. He doubted the hospital would do anything to him, but they might rescind Georgia's job offer if she caused trouble so soon after being hired back again.

"Yes, you should have. But you need to tread carefully around Mueller. He's not someone to mess around with. He's lodged complaints against several other staff members."

"I don't give a damn who he is or how many complaints he's lodged. If I hear of him doing what he did yesterday again, I might lodge a complaint of my own."

Eli didn't laugh this time, but he did smile. "You might want to wait until your official start date before doing anything like that. You might just find yourself booted out on your rear."

She smiled back at him, and it was as if the last words she'd lobbed at him during the breakup hadn't held the sting he'd thought they'd had. "My rear's pretty tough, actually. And I don't normally stay down."

"Of that I'm sure."

Her smile slowly faded, and they sat there staring at each other for seconds that grew painfully awkward. At least on his side. And he probably shouldn't have said what he had, because the words had been pretty loaded and he had no doubt she'd read between the lines. Had he meant her to?

Probably.

"You didn't stay down for long either, evidently." Then she shook her head. "Sorry—that was uncalled for. I'll let you get back to what you were doing. I just wouldn't have felt right if I didn't at least try to get your opinion."

Her cryptic comment about him not staying down for long hit home. And she wasn't wrong, if she was referring to him and Lainey. But just like the patient, there was nothing he could do about that now. And as for his opinion on said patient, he realized he hadn't given her one. Because he couldn't. A suddenly racing heart could be caused by so many things. Some of them benign and some of them deadly. "I'll tell you what. If the patient comes back in and you're here, call me and I'll come down."

"I gave her my phone number. If she calls me, would you be willing to talk to her? Since you have a private practice in addition to your work at the hospital, I mean. You could do that, right—without it causing problems between you and Mueller?"

"Nowadays I normally need a referral, but yes, I would talk to her and offer to dig a little deeper into her symptoms. Does that help?"

"It does." She passed a slip of paper to him. When he opened it, he saw the name *Molly Breckin*. "That's the patient. And Eli...thank you. I mean it."

With that she got up and walked out of his office the same way she'd walked in: with softly swaying hips and without any fanfare. But it dug into his composure just as much as when she'd first arrived. And long after she was gone, he sat staring at the name on the paper and wondering exactly what he was going to do.

Not about the patient, but about Georgia. About the way she affected him without even trying. With no answers in sight, he opened the top left drawer of his desk and dropped the slip of paper inside, but not before committing the woman's name to memory.

Why was Georgia so relieved that Eli had taken her seriously? Had she really expected him to throw her out of his office with a few harsh words? Maybe. And it could be that she deserved them. But why? She'd been true to her heart three years ago. How could anyone fault her for that? And if she'd known that Eli had been dead set on marriage when they'd first started dating she probably would have never gone out with him.

But how many men—or women, for that matter—expected to date someone indefinitely without any hope for the relationship to deepen and mature?

Evidently she'd been living in la-la land. But not anymore. If there'd been any doubts that he could accept anything less in a relationship than marriage, those should have been put to rest when Eli had ended up marrying someone else a year after their breakup. So to think he would have been satisfied with merely sharing a bed and some pretty words was a little ludicrous.

But that was exactly what she'd hoped. Oh, she'd loved him, of that there was no doubt. She'd even said the words from time to time. But she hadn't wanted or needed a ring to go with that love. And when he'd acted like she had to have one for their relationship to continue? She'd checked out. Both physically and emotionally.

However, right now, it was time for her to go to her apartment and have a nice long bath and a glass of wine and try to forget about Molly Breckin and Eli Jacobsen. She wasn't sure it was possible, but she'd better try if she was going to have the courage to show up for work tomorrow. And the day after that. Otherwise, she might as well pack her bags and head back to Kodiak.

As soon as she got to the ER the next morning, she was met with a mess. There were several ambulances in the bay.

She caught up with William. "What happened?"

"A floatplane carrying a group of campers lost engine power on the way to Katmai National Park and made a hard water landing. The passengers and pilot had to ditch the plane. We're still waiting on three passengers, but the other four were picked up from the water and choppered in. Thank God the company followed the regulations for personal flotation devices."

"For sure. Serious injuries?"

"Actually yeah, a couple. You'd think that a crash involving water would be softer, but we've got a possible ruptured spleen. That patient has been transported to surgery. And we've got several broken bones. Also a pregnant lady is having abdominal pains. We're waiting on her."

"Okay, send me where you need me."

Just then a pair of EMTs pushed through the door with a woman holding her distended abdomen in a way that could only mean she was carrying a baby. That answered that question.

"I'll take her to a room," Georgia said. "Has Labor and Delivery been notified?"

"Yes. But there are two emergency deliveries going on up there, and they're swamped. If we can get her stabilized until they can send someone down, that's the preference. If it's dire, we'll take the gurney up there."

"Got it. Thanks."

She glanced at the big whiteboard to see if

there were any exam areas open. "Okay, let's take her to room six."

Georgia hurried over to the woman. "I'm Dr. Sumter. We're going to get you into a room where I can take a look at you. Any trouble breathing?"

The young woman had to be in her early twenties. "No, but my stomach hurts and my baby…" Her eyes closed. "I can't feel her, and I'm so scared."

"I know you are. I know you're wet from being in the water, but can you feel any kind warm flow down there?"

"No."

Hopefully that meant there was no bleeding and the uterus hadn't been compromised. Intake wristbands were often color-coded during triage as an aid in the order patients were seen, but those scales weren't always reliable when it came to expectant women, so Georgia just took her straight to an exam room.

One of the EMTs handed her a chart. The woman's name was Lydia.

"Lydia, were you struck in the stomach by anything?"

"I—I don't think so. But everything happened so fast. We had our seat belts on when we hit the water."

"Was the belt low? Like down here?" She motioned to the area at the base of her abdomen.

"Yes."

"Okay, good. I'm going to help you out of your clothes and get you into a dry gown. Then we'll make sure the baby's heartbeat is still strong. How far along are you?"

The patient shuddered, probably from the chill of being in the water and in an ER that was kept cool on purpose. Most people complained of being cold while there. "Four months."

"Camping at Katmai is pretty rugged, isn't it?"

"Yes, but my doctor said it was still early enough to—"

Georgia laid her hand on the woman's arm. "I wasn't criticizing. I only meant that I've often thought about going to see the bears but haven't made it up there yet."

"This will be our third time going."

Her attention went on high alert. "Were you with someone? A relative?"

"My husband. They didn't have enough room for him on the first trip and he wasn't seriously injured, so he'll be here as soon as they can get another helicopter to pick him up."

Lauren Adams, one of the nurses who'd been here three years ago, came in and helped Georgia get their patient out of her wet clothing. "It's so good to see you back," she said.

"It's good to be back."

Lydia's undergarments showed no staining that looked like blood. Hopefully a good sign. "Any ETA on Obstetrics getting here?"

"They're both still tied up in surgeries."

"Got it. Let's go ahead and set up an ultrasound then, and if you can make sure the front desk is on the lookout for her husband " She glanced at Lydia. "What's his name?"

"Mark. Mark Jones."

Georgia continued her instructions. "If we could get Mark in here as soon as he arrives, that would probably be helpful for all concerned parties."

"On it." Lauren popped out of the room.

She came back in a minute or two later, wheeling the ultrasound machine. "Where do you want this?"

"How about on the right?"

They got the machine set up, and Lauren typed in the patient's info while Georgia got a tube of lubricating jelly and squirted some on the transponder. She paused. "This is going to be a little cold, okay?"

Lydia nodded.

She squirted some onto the woman's abdomen, then glanced up at Lauren. "Are you ready for me?"

"Yep, go ahead."

She pushed the wand through the lubricant and used it to spread the gel around the area she wanted to scan. Then she pressed into the firm bulge and watched the screen, praying to hear a heartbeat that sounded normal and see structures that looked typical for this stage of pregnancy.

There was silence in the room, then Lydia winced when Georgia hit an area low on her belly.

"What is it?"

"I don't know. It's just really sore there." The area was right about where Lydia had indicated the seat belt would have sat.

"Okay, I'll try to be careful. Let me know if anything else hurts." Georgia prayed that was all the pain was from.

When she still couldn't find the heartbeat, she tensed. "Let me move to the other side."

"Is everything okay?" Lydia's voice was a little softer, her concern evident.

"I think the baby is just positioned differently." She tried to reassure the patient the best she knew how, but she was beginning to worry as well.

Standing over her, Georgia added more lubricant and then began a sweep of the new area. Still nothing.

Just as she was getting ready to move to a third area, she heard something and backed the transponder up.

There.

Lub-dub, lub-dub, lub-dub.

"Thank God." Lydia's whispered words threaded through the room. Georgia echoed them. And when she looked over at Lauren, she caught the nurse swiping at her eyes. She got it. She felt a little emotional as well. How would she feel if that was her on the exam table praying for everything to be okay with her baby?

Well, that wasn't a possibility, since she didn't think she would ever be a mother, since she didn't want a "forever" relationship. Not with a man, not with anyone.

Including having a child of her own?

She didn't know. She'd never really thought about it. Until now. But she really didn't think she had it in her to raise a baby on her own. She'd seen how hard her mom had had to work to provide for her after her dad had left. But despite that, Georgia had to admit her mom had seemed to come into herself. Becoming someone different than she had been. Happier. More confident.

She'd even led a support group, helping other women who were trapped in risky relationships. Georgia had gone to one of the meetings once to support her mom, and what she'd heard there had firmed up her belief that marriage was not for her.

"The baby's heart sounds good and strong. I'm just going to take a look at a few other things, if you're okay with it?"

"Oh, yes. I just need to know that everything's okay."

Now that the immediate crisis of knowing the baby was alive was over, Georgia took her time and pointed out various things on the screen. While they were looking, the baby seemed to turn its head to look toward them before its hand clumsily came up and stayed near its mouth. "I think he or she is sucking their thumb."

The miracle of carrying a baby had never ceased to fascinate her. So much so that she'd almost specialized in obstetrics, but something had stopped her—maybe her childhood trauma. Whatever it was, she felt like sticking with her original plan of being an ER doc was the right decision. She loved the variety of patients and the fast pace, not to mention heartwarming moments like this, when a quiet joy was all that was needed to make the rest of her day a good one.

"I think so too," said Lydia.

Just then the door opened and a man rushed in. "Lydia, are you okay?"

The woman burst into sobs, and the man's gaze shifted to Georgia, the panic in his eyes unmistakable.

"Everything's fine with the baby, as far as I can see," she was quick to reassure him.

He grabbed a chair and pulled it over to his wife and laid his cheek against hers. "It's okay, love. I'm here now."

"You must be Mark?"

When he looked up and nodded at her, Georgia smiled. "Are you okay? Were you injured?"

"No. Just my thumb, but it's fine." He held

it up and showed her an ugly gash that went up the side.

"Hmm... I think that might need a stitch or two. And after being in the water, it also warrants a tetanus shot, just to be safe."

"Anything—as long as Lydia and the baby are okay."

"I still want the folks up in Obstetrics to check her out when they finish up with their emergencies, so you may be in for a little wait. Is that okay?"

"Absolutely."

"I'll get you stitched up while you're in the room, and I'm sure someone from the front desk will want to come and get some information from you, but you both were very lucky."

"I know we were."

Lydia wiped her eyes and pulled her husband down for a quick kiss before looking at Georgia again. "Thank you so much."

"You're very welcome." She wiped the transponder down with an alcohol wipe and handed it to Lauren, who took care of the rest. "We'll get you cleaned up and then patch your husband up, and once you're cleared by one of our obstetricians you can go on and enjoy your vacation."

Lydia gripped her husband's hand and

looked at him. "Is it okay if we just go home and watch a documentary on bears instead?"

Everyone in the room laughed, breaking up what had been a nerve-racking half hour.

"Absolutely," Mark said. "And thanks again."

"Not a problem. Now, let's work on getting you cleaned up."

Forty-five minutes later, Mark had been stitched and given a tetanus shot and one of the OB-GYN docs had arrived to take over Lydia's case.

It left Georgia free to exit the room and see what was next on the plate. But it was eerily still all of a sudden. William was nowhere to be seen either.

She went up to the front desk. "Any other crash victims that need to be seen?"

"Nope—they've all been either discharged or moved to other areas of the hospital for further treatment."

"Okay." When she glanced at her watch, she was surprised to see it was one in the afternoon, and her stomach was grumbling. "Are you okay if I run to the cafeteria for a quick bite?"

"Yep, I think we're good."

"Okay, call me if you need me. I shouldn't be any longer than a half hour or so."

"Take your time and enjoy."

With that, she headed down the hallway that led away from the ER and into the rest of the hospital.

CHAPTER THREE

ELI WAS SITTING in the cafeteria nursing his second cup of coffee after finishing a ham-and-cheese sandwich. He was getting ready to get up to leave when Georgia came through the door.

Damn it. He should have just gotten his coffee to go and been done with it.

She hadn't seen him yet, moving with purpose toward the line and glancing at the offerings.

The ends of her dark hair curled around her face and neck and slid over her shoulders. The style was different from how she used to wear it, but it looked good on her. But so would just about anything.

Her black pants clung to the curve of her bottom and hips, and he could see a sliver of pale skin when she leaned over to reach for something in the refrigerated section of the counter. He swallowed, remembering all too well how that skin felt under his fingertips.

Get up and leave before she sees you.

He started to, but something held him back. Maybe he didn't want to look like a coward if she spotted him slinking away from the table.

But it was hard not to just flee. Like she had three years ago? He thought he might know how she'd felt back then because he wasn't so sure he was up to staying in the same building as her. Lainey had stayed at the hospital for weeks after filing for divorce, and although he'd burned with anger over her betrayal, this was different somehow. Georgia hadn't betrayed him. She'd simply not thought he was worth sharing her future with.

Give it a rest, Eli. You've been over this way too many times.

She paid the woman at the counter and turned with her tray just as there was an explosion of sound, as if something had shattered somewhere in the back of the cafeteria. Probably a dropped plate or glass.

Georgia froze, dropping her tray back onto the counter, her eyes wide and unseeing. Her hand reached up and seemed to grab at something near her neck without finding it. She stood there for several seconds, even as another patron edged around her, glancing at her as he went by.

It was enough to make Eli leave his seat and head toward her. "Hey. Are you okay?"

As if some spell had suddenly been broken, she blinked several times, then turned to look at him. "Oh, I..." Then she shook her head. "I'm fine. It just startled me, that's all."

He didn't ask what had startled her. He knew exactly what it was. What he didn't know was why. His mind went back to a time in his apartment when she'd turned to say something to him and knocked a tumbler off the bar, sending it crashing to the ground, glass flying everywhere.

She'd frozen that time too and had seemed to not want to touch the shards. He'd cleaned it up, but when he'd asked her about it, Georgia had simply blown it off, saying what she'd just said, almost word for word. That it had simply startled her.

Ponto final.

"Here, let me carry your tray."

The fact that she didn't argue with him but simply let him lead her back to his table showed him how deeply she'd been shaken by what had happened.

He set her tray down and slid the chair

across from his out and waited for her to sit down. Then he dropped back into his own chair. "Are you sure you're okay?"

"Absolutely. Don't you ever get startled by sudden sounds?"

Yes, but not like that. The way the other customer had edged around her said that that person hadn't thought it very normal either. "I guess it would depend on what it was from."

Her mouth twisted as if she wanted to say something else, but she didn't. Instead, she took a sip of her tea, the tea bag still in the cup, and sucked down a deep breath. "Thanks. I'm not sure why I reacted like that. Maybe my nerves were just stretched tight from what happened with a patient down in ER a little while ago."

"The floatplane accident? I'd heard we'd gotten some of those patients."

"We actually got all seven of them, if I heard right," Georgia said. "I treated a pregnant woman who, thank God, ended up being fine, but I'd heard there were a couple of seriously injured patients."

"There was a splenectomy done, and what else?"

"Some broken bones and I stitched up a thumb, but I thought for a few seconds that the pregnant patient might have lost her baby. I had a hard time finding the heartbeat the first time around."

"You said it ended up being okay, though?" he asked.

"Yes. The baby was just in a different position than I expected. But he or she was active, and there was no bleeding or contracting of the uterus. She had a sore spot on her lower abdomen, which I suspect was from the seat belt in the plane, but there were no other injuries that I could find. Then her husband arrived and was able to help reassure her."

"The way husbands and wives often do for each other."

She glanced at Eli quickly as if looking for something in his face, but he'd schooled the bitterness out of his features just in time. He hadn't even realized he still harbored those kinds of emotions.

Oh, who was he kidding? Of course he did. The same way he harbored some negative feelings toward Lainey for what she'd done. It was a natural part of failed relationships, right? Georgia probably harbored some ill will toward him as well. After all, she'd left the area, hadn't she? And now she was back. And he wasn't sure why. Not for him, obviously, since there was nothing left of what they used to have.

As if the silence had stretched too long for her comfort, she said, "So how has your day gone? Anything interesting?"

"It's still touch and go with one of my patients from yesterday. I put in a biventricular pacemaker and defibrillator."

"Sounds serious."

In the same way that he didn't know everything about emergency medicine, he shouldn't expect her to know everything about his specialty. "It is, and I'm still not sure she didn't come in too late to be saved. But I'm hopeful, even if I'm not very optimistic."

She smiled. "I remember you being one of the most optimistic people I'd ever met."

He had been. At least back then. He'd thought a kid who'd bounced around foster homes had a chance for a normal life and a normal family. His optimism had had known no bounds. Until reality had come in and dragged it through the mud. But at least being a realist brought with it less chance of disappointment.

"Maybe I'm just more judicious about who I use that optimism on."

"Meaning you won't waste any on me anymore?"

"I didn't say that." But he might have thought it. And she'd as much as caught him.

Georgia shrugged. "So your patient with the pacemaker—how long before you know if the surgery worked or not?"

"The surgery worked, but I'm just not sure her heart won't give out despite the surgery. The next twenty-four to forty-eight hours are critical. In reality, I don't know what kind of quality of life she'll have. And a lot of it will depend on how much she wants to live. I felt like she was resigned to her fate when her family asked her to try one more specialist."

"You?"

"Yep. I drew the short straw. Or maybe—if she lives—they'll see it as the right straw. It was the only hope I could offer her."

"Some hope is better than none, though."

Was it? Sometimes hope kept you hanging on to something that was dead and gone.

He decided to answer in terms of his patient rather than himself. "Her family sure hopes so."

"Well, I hope she makes it."

"So do I."

He glanced at her plate, realizing she'd

eaten almost all of her lunch, although it had consisted of yogurt and granola that she'd mixed together to form a meal. And his coffee was now cold and bitter. He could think of nothing less appealing than that. So best to cut his lunch hour short.

"Well, I'd better head back upstairs. I have some phone calls to make and patient records to update." He paused as a thought came to him. "No word on your mystery patient from yesterday?"

"No, not a peep. If she decides to call or come back in, you'll be the first one I notify."

Eli stood. "Sounds good. I'll see you later."

"See you." She got up as well, uncurling those long legs and standing, shaking her dark hair away from her face as she held her tray, her green eyes on his as if she couldn't look away a second or two.

Then she turned and headed in the opposite direction, and he realized that was one thing that no one could contest about what she'd just said, despite his hopes for the contrary: They would indeed see each other later. Whether they wanted to or not.

There was no doubt about it, Eli had changed. She couldn't say whether it was a good change or a bad one. He was just different from the man she'd once known. She hadn't lied when she'd said he'd been the most optimistic person she'd known. But she couldn't say that now. At least not from the little of him she'd seen over the last three days. Yesterday at the café that point had been driven home. His attitude about his patient had held almost a fatalistic air that she never would have equated with Eli Jacobsen. He'd said he was hopeful but not optimistic.

She'd woken up this morning still thinking about that. She hadn't seen much hope in his attitude about his patient's surgery. Maybe it was a reference to that particular patient rather than a complete shifting of Eli's personality.

She hoped so. It made her sad to think of him as anything other than the guy who'd had a boyish charm that just wouldn't quit. Who'd bowled her over almost from the very beginning, and he'd still bowled her over even as their relationship had been ending.

She still had a picture of him in her mind as he'd come over while she'd stood paralyzed by the crashing sound that had come from somewhere inside the café and asked if she was okay. Those deep blue eyes had been full of concern, and it had made her heart melt. She'd had to steel herself to keep from leaning against him like she might have done in times when they'd still been a couple. She'd never told him why that sound bothered her so much, even when they'd been together, although he'd seen her react more than once to the sound of breaking glass. Maybe because revealing that secret would have made her feel vulnerable in ways that she hated. In ways that reminded her of how her dad had relished making feel exposed and fearful.

She pulled the chain holding her butterfly charm from under her shirt and fingered it, her thumb tracing over the raised lines of the insect's wings. She might have bought it after her breakup with Eli, but she realized it was also symbolic of being free of her dad's abuse. A reminder that she didn't need to rely on anyone. She could fly all by herself.

That there might've been holes in that logic didn't matter. What did matter was that it made her feel powerful and self-sufficient.

Dropping the butterfly back to its hidden spot where it rested against her heart, she smiled and loaded her breakfast dishes into the dishwasher of her little rented studio apartment and went to get ready for work.

Ugh! The second Georgia put her purse in the locker area, she frowned. Had she missed this notice earlier? There was one of the hospital's mass meetings happening over the course of two days starting the day after tomorrow. If she remembered right, it was one of those things where they went over policy changes and so much other minutia that she often found herself nodding off. Eli would either send her a text or squeeze her hand to help keep it from being too noticeable. But she wouldn't have him to lean on this time.

You don't need to lean on anyone, remember?

Lauren came in, sticking her own purse in her locker. She caught Georgia's eye and must have seen something in her face. "You look like you're looking forward to that meeting about as much as I am. They're the worst. Do the people in charge not have advisors to... er, advise them?"

That made Georgia laugh. "It appears not because they've been doing it this way for ages. Including having to sign up for a spot." There were probably ten sheets of lined paper with days and times on it where they were supposed to put their names. "It must be how they make sure everyone has attended it. Can't they just put out a new policy manual with any changes highlighted or something?"

"Naw, that would be too easy, eh? Then they couldn't have their hour at the microphone. I always feel like I'm being held hostage."

Georgia took a closer look at the list and saw that William was signed up for the first day at three o'clock. Rats, she was on shift until five that day, so they couldn't go together. She'd just take the 8:00-a.m. slot and get it over with. She scribbled her name. "When are you going?"

"I'm putting it off until the very last second. That way I can look forward to my day off even more."

"Probably a better strategy than mine."

"We can compare notes when we're done."

She smiled, handing the nurse the pen. "It's a deal."

Georgia had about a half hour to kill, so she went out to the courtyard. It was only useable for part of the year, so she'd always loved coming out here when everything was green and lush. She almost always came before her shift to enjoy it. Like a kind of meditation that prepared her for the frenetic pace that the emergency department sometimes had.

The hospital had planted flowers in huge urns that lined a stone walkway, which in turn led to a gazebo. Rocking chairs were set out in a circle inside its protected space. She couldn't remember how many times she'd come out here to read or eat a salad instead of eating in the cafeteria.

There was only one person in the gazebo, and she prepared to smile a greeting until blue eyes came up and speared hers. Oh, God, of course she would have to come when he was here. She didn't remember this being one of Eli's favorite spots. When he wasn't working, he'd wanted to be away from the hospital, not in it, even if the space was beautiful. She sighed. It was obvious they were going to run in to each other more than she'd hoped. Or maybe that was fate's way of laughing at her.

"Mind if I join you?" What else could she say? *Get the hell out?* That wouldn't stand out as unreasonable at all.

"Please."

It wasn't exactly an invitation, but his inflection hadn't oozed sarcasm, unless she'd missed it. She reminded herself that this Eli wasn't the same person she'd left three years ago.

So she sat down across from him rather than in the rocker beside his. "So are you just coming on duty or going off?"

"I actually got an early start, so I'm kind of between patients right now, and thought I'd come out to get a breath of fresh air."

"You used to just go to the coffee shop across the street."

"That's right. But I don't anymore."

That was a weird way to say it. It was as if something had turned him off the place. She and Eli had gone there occasionally, but it hadn't been "their place," so she didn't see that as being the reason.

Maybe it had to do with his ex-wife. Georgia realized she had no idea if the woman was still at the hospital or not. She and Lainey Grant had never been close friends, but they'd always been cordial to one another. And she'd liked the other woman. She couldn't imagine how Lainey and Eli had gotten together so quickly. But then again, people did strange things. She just wouldn't have expected it of Eli. Had marriage meant that much to him that he'd needed to jump right into it with the next available girl? Maybe the "who" hadn't been as important as the "what"? Maybe marriage had been the end goal...which he'd obviously achieved.

Was she being a little unfair? Probably. So she shifted back to the subject at hand.

"So you come out here now instead?"

"Sometimes."

Okay, so it didn't look like he was in the mood for conversation. Except she remembered something and suddenly had to know. "How is your patient doing? The biventricular-pacemaker one?"

This time he fixed her with a look that made her shiver. "Her kidneys are shutting down."

Those five words carried the weight of the world in them. "Oh, Eli, I'm so sorry. But maybe she'll pull through. Sometimes the shock of a big change like that upsets the balance of things in the body. It might just be trying to adapt to its new normal."

He didn't say anything right away, just looked off into the distance. When he did respond, he simply said, "And sometimes it can't."

Were they still talking about the patient? She couldn't tell. "Do you want to talk about it?"

"Not particularly."

"Okay."

She wasn't sure what to do other than to sit there in silence, wishing she had some magic quip that could make him feel better or would give him hope. But would that be doing him a favor or just making it harder if his patient did in fact...die?

A couple of minutes went by, then he shook his head. "Sorry. I know I'm not very good company right now."

She looked at him. His short hair looked like a million fingers had been dragged through it, making it stick up at odd angles. She remembered that from when they'd been together, from when he'd really been troubled about something. He was leaning forward, elbows on his knees, hands dangling in front of those. Strong hands. And yet they were hands that wrought work that was both delicate and amazing. Georgia knew she was good at what she did, but she couldn't reach inside someone and coax their heart to beat again. He'd once performed that miracle on her own heart, coaxing it to beat to its own rhythm rather than forcing it to match his own. Above all, he'd never once made her feel afraid.

So why had she left?

Because she'd needed to know that she was good on her own. She'd had a series of boyfriends through high school and beyond. Things had always been fun and easy until those guys had wanted a deeper commitment. And every time it had happened, something inside of her had churned, making her feel like agreeing to any of those things meant subjugating herself to someone else's will. After all, wasn't that what a proposal was? Asking someone to stay with them? Forever?

But it had never before been hard to end things. She'd always felt a freedom in doing that. A freedom that reiterated again and again that she had the power to say no. At least that was how it had always been. Until Eli. Leaving him had shocked her system, much like she'd talked about with his biventricular patient, and she wasn't sure her heart had ever really recovered. It was why she'd bought herself that butterfly charm. To remind herself why she'd left. To remind herself that her freedom was important, even when there was a terrible price to be paid for it. And maybe, on some level, Eli had paid the price for her need as well. And for that she was sorry. Truly sorry.

Something made her reach out and touch one of those strong hands. "Hey, it's fine. I'm not always the best company either."

He nodded, glancing up at her. "Did you hear from Dr. Mueller's patient?"

The question took her by surprise. "Dr. Mueller's... Oh, right—Molly Breckin, the heart-racing patient. No, unfortunately I haven't heard a peep. But I hope, even if I never hear from her, that she doesn't give up. That she keeps looking for answers until she finds them."

Like Georgia had done with her own quest for independence? She'd been so sure that she knew the answer to that. And yet, right now in this moment, like Dr. Mueller's patient, she wasn't so positive that the answer she'd found had been the right one.

Her eyes met Eli's, and something in her heart stirred. Swallowing, she let go of his hand and raised her arm to press the butterfly charm into the skin beneath her shirt, reminding herself again of why she'd done what she'd done.

Dropping her hand, she glanced at the watch on her wrist, catching sight of the scar just below the band. A half hour was up. Time to leave. "Well, I need to get back to work. I do hope your patient makes it, no matter how grim it looks right now."

"Thanks. I hope she does as well."

Georgia stood to her feet. "See you later." Then she turned and moved away from him, each step taking her farther and farther from him. As she did, she did her best to push the thought from her mind that this felt like another time—one in the past—when she'd walked away from him and never looked back.

CHAPTER FOUR

THE CONFERENCE ROOM was already filled with people, and Eli was glad he'd gotten there in enough time to choose a seat toward the back part of the U-shaped set of tables. These meetings were never fun, but the sooner they got started the sooner he could get back to work.

His biventricular patient had made it through the next two nights, surprising him. She'd even given him a wan smile when he'd visited her room on rounds this morning. Her urine output still wasn't great, and the decision would have to be made soon about dialysis.

Strumming his fingers on the table, he glanced at the clock on the wall. They were already running five minutes late. He was glad when the hospital administrator finally climbed to his feet and walked to the podium.

Just then the doors opened and Georgia entered the room. That made him smile. She was late as usual. She scanned the room, eyes lighting on his for a second and her own lips curving. Oh, hell, she thought he was smiling at her. He quickly schooled his face. Thankfully the chairs on either side of him were already occupied. He wished he would have remembered, though, that they both liked to get these meetings over with, unlike how him and Lainey were at opposite ends of the spectrum.

Looking back, Nicholas, who'd been one of his closest high school friends, had also liked to go to these meetings on the last day, which probably explained where their connection had formed. He'd introduced them, and of course, Nick had been at his wedding, but he'd never suspected anything would come of it.

Lainey had mentioned maybe commuting to work after they'd started dating. But their schedules had never quite meshed enough to do that. Probably foreshadowing what was to come. And looking back, Eli could now see the jump from friendship and sympathy to fiancée had happened far too quickly. He'd probably been trying to fill the void that Georgia's leaving had created.

And although Lainey had been all in, bringing up the subject of commitment before he'd really had a chance to think things through, he'd allowed himself to be swept along in the stream of her apparent happiness, justifying to himself that this was what he'd wanted with Georgia. He'd even convinced himself that maybe Georgia wasn't "the one," maybe Lainey was, since she'd seemed to want what he had: marriage and a family. He'd thought things would be okay, but of course they weren't, and it had soon become apparent that they were two different people with conflicting expectations. She'd needed constant reassurance that she was his all in all. And it had become harder and harder to give that to her as time had gone on.

But from all accounts she was happy now. She had stayed at the hospital after the divorce for a while before she and Nick had moved out to one of the Aleutian Islands, where they both worked at a small clinic.

Eli shook himself from his thoughts, glancing over again at Georgia. She sat in one of the only two seats left available, directly across from him on the other side of the U. Was that any better than her sitting next to him? Yes. Because he could remember a time during just such meetings when they'd sit side by side, their hands clasping beneath the table, his thumb unable to resist stroking across her warm palm. It was amazing how a simple touch could turn him on like it had. But then when it came to Georgia, just a look from her could make him hard and ready. No one else had gotten to him the way she had, not even Lainey. Looking back, he'd been lucky Georgia had left when she had because if she'd done what Lainey had done and found someone else, it would have destroyed him.

And her leaving hadn't?

Something he wasn't going to think about right now. He realized he was still staring at her when her glance swung from where the hospital's administrative director was talking about the latest fundraising campaign to him. Eli blinked back to awareness for a second time and turned his attention back to the speaker. These meetings were always the same. Talking about stuff that could have been done through their company email. There was a 5K walk/run planned for later in the summer, they were all encouraged to participate.

Running had never been one of Eli's passions, despite the fact that Georgia loved it. Eli's biggest passion had been his job. And later, his cabin. One that he'd built with his own two hands. He had bought some land forty-five minutes outside of Anchorage ten years ago, thinking when he eventually got married, he and his wife could put a house on it. But in the dark days after Georgia had left, the thought of doing something for himself on that land had consumed him.

So after getting drunk one night and needing Lainey to drive him home, he'd taken a two-month leave of absence and decided to build an off-grid cabin there instead of a family home. Cutting the timber and peeling the logs had been one of the ways he'd gotten through that time. It had been therapeutic in a way nothing else could have been. Lainey had appeared with food, coffee, and a listening ear whenever she'd had a day off. He'd come to look forward to her visits, since it had taken his mind off his own morbid thoughts.

Steve, his close friend and mentor, had also come periodically and helped him do some of the heavier work, like the loft and putting on the roof, and he'd given Eli some advice he'd never taken: to give Georgia a few months to think about things and then try to go talk to her.

It was only then that he realized he'd never actually met her mom. He knew she'd grown up in the city of Kodiak on Kodiak Island, but she'd never mentioned her dad, and when he'd asked one time she'd simply said he wasn't a part of her life.

He glanced at her again. Having parents that weren't part of your life anymore was something he'd become painfully conscious of after the automobile crash that had ripped his own from him in a slash that had taken a long time to get over. It was funny how few foster parents wanted to be saddled with a grieving teenager who acted out from time to time. So he'd bounced from one house to another until he'd finally landed at Steve Davis and his wife's home. Steve had just been starting his medical practice but had taken time away from it to spend with Eli, going with him to get therapy and letting him shadow him at work. It had been exactly what he'd needed, and it was a big part of the reason Eli was now a doctor.

The sight of hands going up all over the room made him realize that the man at the podium had asked about something. He wasn't sure if it was a vote or if it was just to get opinions on something. Georgia's hand had gone up, and when she glanced at him, her brows went up as if in surprise.

He asked his neighbor what he'd missed,

and it was evidently a question about whether they would like to see more money put into the cardiac department. It was too late to put his hand up now, but he was pretty sure he was going to be asked about it later.

Time to really start paying attention before something else slipped by him. So for the remainder of the meeting he forced himself to keep his eyes on the front of the room and his mind off of the past—and more importantly—off of Georgia.

Then it was over, thank God, and people started getting up, including him. But just as his eyes met Georgia's again, the administrator called his name over the microphone. "Dr. Jacobsen... Eli...could I pick your brain about something for a minute?"

Oh, hell, busted. Still looking at Georgia, he saw her eyes sparkle, and her brows waggled in a way that said she wouldn't want to be him right now. Then she left the room.

She wasn't the only one who didn't want to be him, as he caught several sympathetic glances as people walked by him. Even Eli didn't want to be him right now.

Gathering his thoughts, he moved toward the podium. And met Marcus Adams, making sure they weren't near enough to that microphone that they could be overheard.

The administrator shook his hand. "I'm curious about something. Is there a reason you wouldn't want to see your department grow or have more money dedicated to it?"

Eli's brain whizzed through ideas and finally came up with something that sounded plausible enough. "I'd want to see what the ideas were before committing to them. I don't want to see growth that comes too fast and isn't sustainable."

Like his marriage to Lainey?

No. This really was about the hospital. He'd seen that very thing happen from time to time, when they either couldn't hire enough staff to cover the rapid growth or there weren't enough patients to justify it. The latter wasn't something he saw happening, but good staffing wasn't always an easy thing to come by. And bad staffing… Ronny Mueller immediately came to mind.

"Okay, that's what I thought. I'll make sure to run our ideas by you before we make any hard and fast decisions. Does that ease your concerns?"

"It does. Thank you, Marcus."

"Thank you for running one of the best cardiac units in all of Alaska."

"There are a lot of people involved in running the department. I couldn't do any of it without them."

The man gave him a smile that Eli was pretty sure didn't mean anything. It was just that of a politician looking for votes so he could push his agenda through. Then he pulled himself up short. No, that wasn't really fair. The man was good at his job. This hospital had flourished because of some of the changes Marcus had made when he'd come aboard seven years ago.

"I'll send you some of my thoughts over the next couple of days," Marcus said. "When you have time, if you could get back to me on them, I'd appreciate it."

"I will. And thanks again."

"Not a problem. Thanks for coming to the meeting."

All Eli could do was smile, because it hadn't been an optional gathering. But at least he would get something in writing before the department was handed a big check without any concrete plans for what the money was supposed to go toward.

He headed for the door just as some of the

next group made their way to their seats. One of his colleagues caught him before he made it out. "How was it?"

"About the same as it always is."

"That's what I was afraid of. Thanks."

Eli finally got out of the room and spied Georgia talking to William just across the corridor. The other man's eyes clipped his for a second before ending whatever conversation he'd been having with his friend and sliding through the door. But not without sending a nod in Eli's direction as he did.

Georgia came over. "Did you get in trouble?"

He couldn't stop a chuckle when she made it sound like they were still in school. "I didn't get detention, if that's what you mean."

"I thought he might make you sit through the meeting again." Thankfully she didn't ask him why he'd been staring at her through much of the hour.

"No, but he did ask why I wasn't in favor of growing my department."

"Oh, boy. I bet that was awkward."

He smiled again. "Only a little. Listen, do you want to get some coffee, or do you need to get back?"

"My break was supposed to happen after

the meeting, so I have about a half hour. How about that coffee shop across the way?" Then she stopped short. "Or we could just go to the cafeteria."

Did she know why he avoided that coffee shop? No, how would she? He was pretty sure what had happened there had never made it through the hospital rumor mill.

The day that he'd walked into the shop and caught Lainey and Nick sitting at a table holding hands had been the day his marriage had ended. Lainey had tried to babble an explanation, only Eli hadn't been interested. He wasn't proud of his reaction. He'd simply unscrewed the wedding ring from his finger and walked over to the table and dropped it on the table in front of her. Then he'd walked out, moving his stuff out of their apartment before she'd gotten back. They'd never spoken again, except through their divorce lawyers, despite the fact that they'd both still been working at Anchorage Memorial.

The one thing he'd fought hard for had been his cabin, which she'd told her lawyer she'd wanted, even though once they'd been married she'd never expressed any interest in it again. Despite having visited the site during the building phase, she'd always acted like she was above staying in such a rugged place. Fortunately, she'd settled for money instead.

Realizing Georgia was waiting for his answer, Eli said, "The coffee shop is fine." He hoped to hell she wasn't going to start trying to be his friend because the time for that was long gone. And the last thing he thought he could manage was to get past everything that had happened and slip into an easy—and platonic—relationship with her. Because despite everything, the last thing he felt toward Georgia was anything approaching platonic. He'd proved that by the memories that had risen up during the staff meeting.

They walked across to the coffee shop, and when they pushed the door open a bell rang, announcing their arrival. He didn't remember that being there a couple of years ago. Had they put it up after he'd caught Lainey and Nick together to warn others who might be meeting in secret that someone was arriving?

Now, that was being paranoid.

The tables had been rearranged or replaced as well. The area where his ex and Nick had sat was now set up like a conversation area, with a circle of comfortable chairs and a few low-slung coffee tables. There were high café tables and barstools over on the left side of the shop. Despite the line of people waiting to place their orders, there were still plenty of spots left to sit, so most folks were probably taking their beverages with them.

The lighting in the place was low, with swagged lines of bare bulbs providing a casual but intimate ambience that made him slightly uncomfortable, although if it affected Georgia, he wasn't seeing it.

They got in line, and Eli was surprised when it moved quickly. "What are you getting?"

Her eyes were up on the menu. "And iced vanilla latte, I think."

He remembered she liked those cold caffeinated drinks. In fact, even when they'd been together she would sometimes make coffee and then take her time drinking it. Sometimes she'd even forgotten where she'd left her cup and once she'd found it would drink the rest of it cold, laughing when he'd made a face at her. He preferred his coffee hot.

He also preferred his coffee strong and black.

They placed their order, and the barista gave them a little plastic number to set up at whatever table they chose.

They went over to one of the high café tables, and Georgia climbed onto her stool. "I'm kind of afraid to ask, but did your patient make it?"

He didn't need to ask which patient she was talking about. "Yes. Her numbers are slightly better today, although there's still a possibility she'll need dialysis. But there's been a definite improvement."

"I told you that could happen."

"You did, but I've found it's best to be prepared in case things don't work out like you expect them to."

She looked down at the table for a few seconds before glancing back at him. "Are you talking about your patient? Or about something else?"

He nodded to acknowledge that she'd read the situation correctly. "It can apply to almost anything. Including my patient."

She didn't ask about his marriage, but she'd probably already deduced that it fit in that category as well.

"How about growing your department? Does that fit in there too?" This was said with a smile, and he let one side of his mouth kick up.

"Like I told the administrator, I don't want

them going too fast and jumping ahead of themselves."

And just like that, he realized that's probably what he'd done with Georgia back when they'd been together. They'd been dating for three years when he'd realized he wanted to spend the rest of his life with her. His proposal had been impulsive, and he saw how she could have been shocked by it. They'd never really discussed the future outside of short-term plans. And they'd not even moved in together. It was no wonder she'd walked out on him. But surely it couldn't have come as a complete surprise that he'd want to get married at some point?

But then again, she'd never gotten married in the intervening time, unlike Eli, who probably appeared to have marriage as the end goal of every relationship. Looking at some of his colleagues, he'd discovered that not all of them chose to get married. Some lived together for long periods of time, having families and raising them together as partners rather than husband and wife. He didn't begrudge them that. He'd just always equated family to what he'd thought was the gold standard—a husband, a wife and a couple of kids.

But marriage didn't guarantee a couple

would stay together. He'd known that in his head, but his heart had wanted it all. And yet that hadn't worked out either.

He could look back and see that he'd probably used Lainey as a substitute for Georgia. And it was something he wasn't proud of. Marriage had been his and Lainey's end goal when it probably shouldn't have been. And because he'd been so devastated when Georgia had left, he'd been less liberal about saying the niceties like *I love you* to Lainey—who seemed to have a deep need for those signs of affection. It was no wonder she'd found someone else to say those things to her instead. He wasn't even unhappy for her. Not anymore.

"Penny for your thoughts."

No way. "They're not even worth that much." He forced a smile and decided to change the subject. "So how are you liking being back at Anchorage Memorial?"

"I love it." She made a little face. "Well, most of it. Dr. Mueller still baffles me. He acts as if he doesn't even *like* his patients. And if I can see it, I'm sure they can too. Why does he even practice medicine? Surely it's not a good look for the hospital."

"Hundreds of thousands of dollars in student loans, maybe? I'll also admit that the hospital wants physicians who are not only good at what they do but who are fast. They feel they can skimp a little on bedside manner if they're excellent and fast, but if not..." Eli shrugged. "I'm not sure why he doesn't change specialties if emergency medicine ended up not being all he'd hoped it would be."

"Maybe he's good at what he does, but I sense from the nurses that he's too quick to let patients walk out of the hospital without a thorough workup. He probably saves the hospital a few bucks on those folks who don't have insurance, but if they have to come back in with the same complaint, then it causes a distrust of our profession. I saw that with Molly Breckin, who'd been dismissed by more than just our hospital."

"Sometimes when it's something that's more difficult to diagnose, things can fall through the cracks."

She gave him a frown. "Would *you* have sent her back out with only an EKG?"

Well, she had him there. "You know I wouldn't have."

"And that's exactly what I mean. Even if it turns out that it's something benign, knowledge is power, and the more information and reassurance a patient gets that tells them you don't think they're crazy, the more often they can settle into their body the way it is." Georgia paused for a minute. "My mom has a prolapsed mitral valve that has given her fits ever since she was a teenager. She was hyperaware of every skipped beat and every blip of irregularity in her heartbeat. But it was only after her divorce that she sought medical advice, and she said her doctor was great and took the time to not only diagnose her but to help her understand what was happening and give her the tools to deal with it. He put her on a beta blocker, and it was a game changer for her. It evened out her heart rate and let her feel like she had her life back."

This was more information than she'd ever given him about her family. It was on the tip of his tongue to ask about her father again, but if she hadn't been willing to share anything about him when they'd been together, it was unlikely she would confide in him now. And it was none of his business, even though Georgia knew pretty much everything about his life in foster care and about Steve being the person who—probably like her mom's beta blockers—had given him his life back.

So rather than going back through any of that, Eli simply said, "I'm glad for her. She still lives on Kodiak?"

"Yep. She probably always will. It's where her mom and grandmother were from, and she places a lot of value on that."

He wondered if her dad was still there as well, but again, he wasn't going to ask. "It makes sense that you went back there, then."

As soon as the words were out of his mouth, he realized he really had no business mentioning that. Once they'd stopped being a couple, she'd probably felt her life was her own again. Maybe leaving him had given her that. "I'm sorry if being with me made you feel any less than you are."

Her eyes widened, and she reached over to touch the hand that wasn't holding his coffee cup. "Oh, Eli, it didn't. I—I just…couldn't. Making that kind of commitment doesn't work for me."

How could she even know that without trying? And she'd never given him any alternatives that she *could* accept, although back then he'd been dead set on marriage and probably would have been unhappy with anything less than that. And now that he'd tried marriage and had it fall in ruins around his feet?

Disillusionment was too soft a word for how he felt about it now.

Despite that, commitment was still important to him. Important enough that he hadn't dated since his divorce because he wasn't sure he would fare any better the next time. So he'd decided that he would just stay single until he could untangle some of those threads.

"I think I get that now. Thank you for not just going along with it for the sake of keeping the peace." Something he'd done with Lainey? Ugh. He needed to stop comparing the two situations. They were miles apart. He glanced at his watch and saw that forty-five minutes had gone by in a flash. "You probably need to be back at work, don't you?"

She glanced at the wall where there was a big clock. "Oh, heavens, yes. I'm already late."

He gathered their trash and flashed her a smile. "Some things never do change, it seems."

"Maybe not. But I just keep trying." She hopped off her stool. "Thanks for the coffee, Eli. And the conversation."

Yeah, he was kind of glad they'd cleared

the air about at least a few things from their past. Did it mean they could forge a new path from here and be colleagues who didn't actively avoid each other?

The jury was still out on that. But he hoped they could.

CHAPTER FIVE

"CALL AND SEE if Dr. Jacobsen can come."
Georgia's words were not a request.

Dr. Mueller shook his head, a stubborn set
to his jaw. "I think we can handle this."

Oh, no. He was not going to bulldoze her
just because he thought he had some kind of
seniority over her. Okay, well, he might tech-
nically have that, but he was wrong about the
rest of it. And she was not about to let another
patient be pushed aside by him.

"Can I speak with you outside for a minute?"

They had a sixty-two-year-old woman
whose EKG was all over the place, sending
flurries of PVCs across the tracings as well as
two episodes of tachycardia within the space
of a couple of minutes. Plus she had a history
of heart failure and was having trouble catching her breath—the latter of which was what
had brought her to the ER. These were not

symptoms they could just ignore. Or at least Georgia couldn't.

Once they were in the hallway, Mueller tried again. "If we just up her dosage of losartan and furosemide, it may pop her back into sinus rhythm and reduce her water retention."

"I don't want to do that without having a cardiologist sign off on it. Her oxygen levels aren't the greatest. And reducing her heart rate even more could send her into bradycardia."

His frown grew stormy. "Look, we're wasting time here. I'm sure Jacobsen would follow the same protocol even if we called him in. She's not my first heart-failure patient."

Maybe not, but Georgia wasn't comfortable with either of the suggestions he'd offered. "Well, why don't we ask him, just to be sure?"

Lauren, who'd been in the room with them, popped her head outside the door and paused for a second as she glanced at their faces. "Is it okay if I go let her husband know she's being treated?" The nurse stared at her, as if looking for a sign, and catching her drift, Georgia gave a slight nod of her head.

"Yes. Go."

Mueller could report her if he wanted to, but if what she thought was happening truly was, then he probably wouldn't dare because it would expose just how little concern he seemed to have for his patients.

Lauren left the room without another word, and Georgia hoped to hell it was to go and ask Eli if he could come and take a look at the patient. She knew William would have gone and immediately checked, but she didn't know Lauren quite as well as she did her childhood friend.

She continued, "I want her to have an echo so we can get a really good look at what her valves are doing and where her heart function currently stands. You can't do that with a simple EKG." She realized her voice had gone up in volume when another nurse came down the hallway where they were standing and gave them a look.

When Mueller didn't answer her, she blew out a breath. "Well, I'm going back in there. Lauren is probably already on the phone with Dr. Jacobsen."

"Why would she call him? Neither of us asked her to. Or did you just…" He drew himself up to his full five foot eight and gave her a baleful look that sent a chill over her. But she didn't back down, matching him scowl for scowl. Finally he threw his hands up in obvious frustration. "Oh, I see how it is. Well, do whatever the hell you want, then. If you're having Jacobsen come down, then I'm not going to waste my time here. I'm going to go treat the next patient in line."

Thank God!

She didn't say the words out loud, but she was pretty sure he could read the relief on her face. In the week and a half she'd been back at the hospital, this was the first real run-in she'd had with Mueller, but he was everything William had told her and more. She couldn't believe the hospital let him go on like he did. But then again, she wasn't the head of the department and she could just about bet that doctor had heard a thing or two about Mueller. But he'd evidently never screwed up enough to be written up or censored. Although Georgia didn't know that for a fact.

She swiveled on her heel and went back through the door to the exam room, leaving the other man standing outside. She hoped to hell he did go to see whatever patient was still out there, who, if Georgia remembered correctly, had hurt their wrist after slipping in the bathtub. She didn't trust Mueller with that any more than she trusted him with their current patient, but at least a wrist injury wasn't life or death.

Within three minutes, Eli strode into the room and took a look at her face and, like he always had, read her like a book. Or maybe Lauren had filled him in. "What have you got?"

"This is Edna Miller. She's short of breath and has a history of heart failure. I really wanted you take a look and maybe set her up for an echo." She handed him the tablet that contained Edna's chart. "Her husband is in the waiting room, hoping for some news."

And he'd thankfully not heard the tense exchange between the hospital's two ER doctors, although Georgia wasn't too sure how soundproof these rooms were. She'd never been in a situation before where she'd felt her blood pressure rise enough to lift her voice to the same level. But if calling in Eli hadn't been the right decision, she didn't know what was. She knew in her gut that upping a patient's meds without exploring things a little further was the wrong decision. She also knew from the huge sense of relief that had washed over her when Eli walked through the door that Edna needed to see the specialist.

She hadn't seen Eli since the coffee shop,

and she, for sure, hadn't sought him out since then. Some of their topics of conversation that day had hit a little too close to home, like him saying he hoped he hadn't made her feel less than she was. Her eyes had burned, and she'd come dangerously close to telling him no, that the only person who had ever done that had been her father. But no one besides her mom, William and their neighbors in the city of Kodiak knew what had happened the day her dad had left for good.

Georgia wasn't sure why she hadn't told Eli when they'd been together other than that she'd learned at a young age to suppress her emotions and hide the details of their life in order to keep the peace with her dad.

Even though she no longer needed to do so, learned behaviors were hard to overcome, as she'd found out when Eli had proposed to her.

As if sensing her thoughts, he looked up from the tablet. But instead of saying anything of a personal nature, he simply said, "I agree with you."

At least she assumed his comment was in regard to their patient.

Their patient.

Well, since she'd called him in, it was true. And since Mueller had washed his hands of the case, at least he had no more say in what happened here.

While Eli went over to talk to Edna about the details of what the echocardiogram would be like, she tried to figure out why Ronny Mueller was the way he was. Was it genuinely that he didn't care, or had the idea that they needed to be as efficient as possible with their time to avoid long waits in the ER become so ingrained that it became automatic? Kind of like her behaviors from childhood. She bet if she looked at Mueller's time-per-patient ratio he would have the fastest times, hands down.

It might've been why he'd been so quick to nudge Molly Breckin to the exit, even though officially she'd been listed as AMA, since she hadn't waited for the discharge paperwork to be signed. That surely worked in Mueller's favor if things went south with her further on down the line.

"Thank you so much, Doctor." Edna's words were choppy and delivered between labored breaths. Even with the supplemented oxygen, she still didn't feel like she was getting enough air. Another reason why Georgia had doubted that simply upping her meds without trying to see exactly what was happening was the wrong choice.

"Do you want your husband here with you?"

"Could I?"

Georgia moved over to the patient's side. "Yes, of course you can. I'll go get him."

Again the sense of relief that Eli was going to do further testing was so strong that she wanted to hug him. Or kiss him.

No matter what, his calm demeanor never left him. Even when she'd broken up with him, he'd never expressed his disappointment in her—when he would have had every right to. They'd dated for a long time. And she'd never once mentioned that marriage was off the table. Mainly because she hadn't known that about herself until the moment he'd asked her to marry him. The horror that had gone through her had been like a tidal wave, and she'd had trouble not turning and running away without giving him an answer. Instead she'd somehow choked one out and then had left him standing there. Alone.

Her heart cramped.

Pulling herself back to the present, she gave him one last glance before leaving the room to get Edna's husband.

Eli had the bedside manner that other doctors only wished they had. He was gentle with his patients, never seeming rushed or hurried in the way he treated them. He'd been the same with her, never seeming to mind spending whatever time it had taken to keep them connected. Only in the end, it hadn't mattered how much time he'd taken, she wouldn't have changed her mind. Maybe she was a little more like Mueller than she liked to believe.

Pushing through the door, she walked down the corridor until she got to the waiting room. Thankfully she didn't run into Mueller on the way.

Edna's husband was the only one in the waiting room at the moment. "Mr. Miller? Would you like to come and be with your wife?"

"Thank you, yes." He got up from his chair, using a cane for extra support as he made his way toward the door. "How is she?"

"About the same. We're going to do a little more testing so we'll know how to make her a little more comfortable." She hoped to hell they could. "But I thought you being there would make her feel better."

"The other doctor didn't seem to want me anywhere near her."

She was careful about how she worded it. Taking away a patient's trust in the medical team could harm the hospital and the doctors who did try to do their best for their patients. And maybe Mueller really had thought upping her medication would help, although something in her soul said otherwise. "We all have our own ideas about what's best for our patients."

He seemed to accept that without question, instead asking, "Do you have any idea why this is happening? Her heart failure seemed to be under control."

"Not yet. But we have a cardiac specialist in there with her at the moment. He'll tell you a little more about our game plan."

"Good. We're actually here on vacation, so her cardiologist is thousands of miles away."

"Really? Where are you from?"

"Florida."

She blinked. "And you came to Alaska?"

"Edna has always wanted to do an Alaskan cruise. And she's loved every minute of it…up until yesterday. The ship's doctor saw her and sent us here to the emergency room."

And Mueller wanted to just up her dose of medications without knowing if it would work while she was thousands of miles away from home? At least with an echo, they would have a better idea of how good or bad her heart function was right now. If the news wasn't good, the couple might have to forgo the rest of their cruise and have Edna admitted for observation. At least until she was stable enough to make the trip back home. Right now, she wasn't. And if they discharged her, she might very well die on the cruise ship.

"He did the right thing," Georgia said. "I'm hoping for the best."

They got to the room, and she pushed the door open to let him go in. Eli was standing next to the bed talking to the patient, who seemed calmer than she had when Mueller had been in charge.

Eli glanced over at Mr. Miller as if including him in the conversation. "I was telling your wife that we have two options for an echocardiogram—which will give us a better visual of how her heart is working. We could start with a handheld unit that I have in my pocket, but my preference would be to do a standard echocardiogram that will give me more information and is displayed on a larger screen."

Mr. Miller went over to Edna and grasped her hand, and they seemed to exchange a look. "We'll go with whatever you think is best."

Edna nodded. "Can Artie stay with me through it?"

"Absolutely," Eli said. "We'll need to move you upstairs to the cardiology unit. I already know I'd like to admit you at least overnight for observation and see if we can get your oxygen levels up."

"But the cruise..." Her eyes watered as she looked up at her husband, who stroked her head.

"There will be other cruises, hon. How can you enjoy this one when it's so hard to breathe?"

"I know."

He leaned over and kissed her cheek. "Let's just get you better, and then we'll talk about the other stuff."

"Okay."

Lauren, who'd come back in the room and overheard the last part of the conversation, said, "I'll go let them know so they can get the paperwork started."

Georgia was pretty sure Dr. Mueller was going to be incensed when he heard, but that was fine by her.

Edna glanced at her. "Can you go with us?"

"I'll need to stay here in the ER in case there are more patients, but I'll try to come up and see how you're doing when I get off work in a couple of hours, okay?" Hopefully Eli would be okay with that, although she was sure she'd hear about it later if she had overstepped her boundaries.

When she looked over at him, there was no expression on his face. No approval or disapproval, so she was going to take that to mean he wasn't vehemently opposed to her entering his domain.

She'd done it before when she'd been at the hospital. It was how she and Eli had gotten to know each other. In fact, when they'd finally started dating, she would go up there under the pretext of checking on a patient when really she'd wanted to see him.

That wasn't the case now, but she cared about her patients. In fact, if Edna couldn't be helped, Georgia was going to feel terrible. She genuinely liked the couple. And they'd been high school sweethearts and had been married for decades.

An orderly came into the room, saying he was here to transport the patient. Georgia went over to the couple and laid a hand on Edna's shoulder. "Dr. Jacobsen is an excellent doctor. There's none better here in Anchorage. If anyone can help you, he can."

When she glanced over at him, she saw he was frowning, although he had given the orderly the okay to take Edna. "I'll be up in a few minutes. I'm just going to call and have them ready to meet you when you get upstairs."

With that, the gurney was wheeled out of the room, with Artie following them, his cane tapping on the floor as he made his way down the hall.

She was pretty sure Eli had something he wanted to say to her, so she hurried to cut him off. "Are you okay with me going to check on her?"

His frown was still there. "Yes, I just wanted to ask if you wanted to be updated on her condition."

She blinked. "Could you do that?" It was something they'd regularly used to do when a patient had been transferred from her department to his, but part of that was because they'd been a couple and she'd been genuinely interested in her patients. Not every specialist wanted to be pestered by an ER doc who was being nosy and wanting to know how someone was doing.

"I could."

"Thank you," she said. "I would really appreciate that. Mueller gave me hell about wanting to call you in. He basically washed his hands of her once he realized Lauren and I were going to override him."

"Lauren?"

"The nurse who called you."

"Ah, that makes sense now." He shook his head. "And don't worry about Mueller. He gets a bug up his butt every time anyone calls for a specialist."

"But why?"

"I have no idea. Delusions of grandeur, maybe?"

"He wanted to just up the doses of her medication."

Eli nodded. "I think I heard he was going on vacation soon, so he'll be out of your hair for a couple of weeks anyway."

"Is it bad that I hope he looks for another hospital while he's gone?"

Eli sighed. "It's getting harder and harder to fire staff, so the administration tries to save that card for serious infractions."

"I would probably argue what constitutes serious."

"Yeah, me too. It's probably why I don't get to make those kinds of decisions. There's a shortage of doctors right now in Alaska, so it's not always an easy task to replace someone."

Was that a jab about her leaving and basically forcing the hospital to hire someone like Ronny Mueller?

And maybe she should feel guilty. She might have made a different decision if she'd known what the consequences would be. Oh, not about turning Eli's proposal down, but about leaving before the hospital had found a suitable replacement. The ER was most hospitals' bread and butter. To be short-staffed in that department was a disaster in the making.

"I get it. I just feel like I have to look over his shoulder now. It's the second time I've heard of or seen him try to get a patient discharged as fast as possible."

"Your young patient?" he asked.

"Yes, Molly Breckin. Although she wasn't my patient. If she had been, she wouldn't have walked out of the hospital without at least talking to a cardiologist."

"Hopefully she'll be back or try another hospital."

"But she shouldn't have had to do either of those two things," she said.

He nodded. "I know, but there's nothing to

be done about it now. We have to take care of the folks who are here now. Speaking of which, I'd better be on my way."

"Okay, sounds good. Thanks for coming down."

"I'll see you a little later, if you come up." He walked toward the door.

"Are you sure you don't mind?"

"I think Edna will be disappointed if you don't come."

No hint of whether he'd be disappointed or not. But then again, why should he feel one way or the other? They weren't together anymore.

"Okay, I'll be up when I get off in a few hours. If you know something before then, you'll call?"

"Yes. I'll call."

He went through the door, and Georgia breathed a sigh of relief. It wasn't as awkward working with him as she'd feared it might be when she'd first thought about coming back to Anchorage Memorial. And while the fact that he wasn't married anymore had filled her with dread when William had first told her, even that hadn't been the catastrophe she'd imagined after she'd heard.

But unless she remained on her guard, it

might become one. Especially if that little nudging voice inside of her didn't let up. It was basically telling her they were both single and so why not let her defenses down a little?

She couldn't. Because if she did, she could very easily fall back into old patterns. And now that she knew where those patterns could lead, she knew she couldn't let herself do that. Because she didn't want what she'd done to him three years ago to ever happen again.

Myocarditis. Both the echo and cardiac MRI showed inflammation of the lower sections of the heart, and Edna had said she'd been pretty sick a few weeks before the cruise. It explained all of her new symptoms like shortness of breath and arrhythmias. A blood test had confirmed she had antibodies for Covid. Myocarditis could be self-limiting and go away on its own, but with Edna's history of mild heart failure, the inflammation could put a strain on the already overworked organ. Thank God Georgia had pushed for the echo. Simply upping her medications wouldn't have helped, and it might have made things even worse.

Eli sat down and came up with a treatment plan, taking into account Edna's existing heart failure, which could complicate treatment. He decided that a round of steroids might knock down the inflammation and allow that portion of the heart to heal. When he was done researching current models, he was fairly confident that his approach was the most likely to succeed. Unfortunately it meant the couple would have to forgo the rest of their cruise so that he could monitor her for a week or so. The only other alternative was to fly her back to the lower forty-nine and wait to start treatment until she got there. But with her shortness of breath, that meant a pretty uncomfortable trip.

He got up from his desk and went to Edna's room in Cardiac Intensive Care, where she had been placed. Once he got there, he found his patient asleep, her husband sitting at her bedside.

The man stood. "Do you know what's causing her symptoms?" His voice was quiet, so as not to wake up his wife, but his face showed how worried he was.

"I have a pretty good idea. The testing we did indicates cardiomyopathy, an inflammation of an area of Edna's heart." Eli pulled out his phone, where there was an anatomical picture of the heart, and waited as Artie put his glasses on. Then he pointed to the area of the heart affected. "We think it was caused by the body's response to when she was sick a few weeks ago."

"You mean her heart has an infection?"

"Not exactly. But her heart reacted to the virus and became inflamed."

"Can it be treated?"

"Yes and no. There's no direct treatment, and antibiotics don't work because it's not an actual infection. What we can do is try to knock down the inflammation with a steroid and give the heart a chance to heal."

"Will the cardio...whatever it is make her heart failure worse?"

"Our goal is for that not to happen. I can't make any hard and fast promises, but the treatment I'm proposing has a pretty good track record as far as that goes. There's one caveat." He paused. "I'd like Edna to stay here while we begin treatment and until she's stable, which means—"

"We can't finish the cruise."

"Unfortunately. That's not to say that you can't go on another one at a later date, but it won't be right away. She'll need three to six months of solid rest so her heart can heal, which means she'll have to limit most of her activities."

"Do you know my wife?"

He shook his head. "No, but I know myocarditis. And while it can go away, strenuous activity runs the danger of putting so much strain on the heart that it causes sudden death."

Artie seemed to blanch. "Sudden death?"

"I'm not saying that would happen, but I want her to have the best possible outcome. I talked to her cardiologist in Florida, and he agrees with me on the treatment protocol and on the time frame."

"Then that's good enough for me. She's been going to him for a long time. Her heart failure had been getting better, which is why her suddenly having these symptoms was so scary."

"Myocarditis, like any inflammation, can come on suddenly. But our goal is for it to cause as little damage as possible," Eli said. "When she wakes up we can go over everything together."

"Is Dr. Sumter able to come up?"

He glanced at his watch. He'd called Georgia about a half hour ago, and she'd said she was just finishing up some last-minute things and then would come up to see the couple. He wasn't sure how he felt about her doing that. It was a throwback to the days when they'd freely shared cases and allowed their personal lives to bleed over into their professional lives. Just like when she'd come to his office last week with the question about Molly Breckin. The more they allowed their lives to overlap now that she was back, the harder it might be for both of them to keep things on a professional level. And one thing he did know was that he wasn't willing for things to move beyond that. Not after the way their relationship had ended.

He was pretty sure that if he allowed them to get involved again—like last time—he couldn't see himself being happy with just dating her for twenty years or longer. And after his and Lainey's divorce, he was pretty sure he wasn't going to want to get married again anytime soon, if ever.

He was pretty happy with his life the way it was right now. It was uncomplicated and easy going back and forth between his apartment and his cabin in the Mat-Su, where he liked to spend most of his days off.

"She should actually be here pretty soon."

"Good. I know Edna will want to see her.

If not for her, I don't know what would have happened. We might be back on that cruise ship out on open water. If something had gone wrong... If something had happened to Edna, I just don't know what I would have done."

"Georgia takes a lot of interest in her patients, so I doubt she'll let you get out of here without visiting at least once or twice."

As if on cue, the door opened and the ER doc walked in. Her glance skipped from him to Artie, who was still on his feet, his cane left beside the bed. "Everything okay?"

Eli nodded. "It's fine. We were just going over treatment options, and I was telling Artie that I want to keep Edna while she's on the steroids, just to monitor how she does on them."

"I think that's a great idea. I'm sorry you won't be able to finish your cruise, though."

Eli had already talked to Georgia about how he'd hoped to proceed as far as the steroids and rest were concerned.

"Edna will be devastated," Artie said, "but I'm willing to do whatever will get her through this."

"It also means I'll be able to come up and see you guys more times." Georgia sent the man a smile.

Eli tensed. He'd expected once or twice... was she actually saying she'd come more than that? He should have realized it, though. He hadn't been lying when he'd said she always took a lot of interest in her patients, probably more than a lot of doctors. She used to have pictures of herself with some of them taped to her locker in the doctors' lounge. Eli had no idea which locker she'd been given this go round, and he purposely had tried to avoid looking for it. He didn't want anything to interfere with his need to keep things with her on a professional basis. And going to look for her locker definitely seemed beyond the purview of doing that.

Edna's voice broke through. "Am I hearing you wrong? I'm going to have to stay in the hospital? And we can't finish the cruise?"

Her voice still sounded breathy and weak, but hopefully a couple of days on the steroids would help with that.

Artie went to her side. "The doctor thinks it's best. And even after we get home, you're going to have to rest for a couple of months."

"Months? But what about our garden?"

"I'll take care of that. You can just give the orders, and I'll carry them out."

Eli couldn't stop a smile of his own. This

was what a partnership was supposed to be, with one person supporting the other when they were at their weakest. A love like this was what he'd hoped to find ever since he'd been a teenager, when he'd felt like a castoff so many times—a burden that nobody had wanted.

Edna grabbed her husband's hand. "Well, ordering you around might not be such a bad thing after all." She took a breath and let it out on a half cough. "I'll be glad when I feel better, though."

"And you will feel better. But it's just going to take some time. I know patience has never been one of your strong suits."

"No, it is not."

That was as emphatic a statement as he'd heard his patient make, and Eli couldn't prevent a smile.

Georgia moved closer to the bed. "It sounds like you're feeling a little better than you were when you came to the ER."

"I am. Because I have answers, thanks to you. I might not even have a treatment plan if you hadn't fought for me."

"Eli was the one who had the game plan. I just knew that you shouldn't go back to the cruise ship in the condition you were in."

Artie sat in the chair beside his wife. "Our son is flying up today and will stay until we're ready to head back to Florida."

"I'm glad you'll have someone to help you get back," Eli said. "And I think we should leave you two alone for a while to plan your garden. That chair you're sitting in pulls out into a bed. We can have sheets and blankets brought in if you want to stay with her."

"I wouldn't want to be anywhere else. Thank you again—for everything."

"My pleasure."

He nodded for Georgia to follow him out. The couple was right. If she hadn't fought for them…if Mueller had been left to his own devices, Edna very well could have died. And Artie would be without his wife and their children would be left without a mom. And while no one at the hospital would ever know it, since she wasn't a local, it still would have been a tragedy that needn't have happened.

This was the Georgia he remembered: Tenacious, fearless, unafraid of standing up to anyone. Even him.

Once they were out of the room, he glanced at her. "Are you off duty?"

"I am." She looked at him for a minute before reaching over to squeeze his hand, much like Artie had done with his wife. "It's moments like the one with that couple that I remember why I wanted to go into medicine."

Her fingers were warm on his skin, and the memory of being able to just hold his hand out and know that she would take it washed over him. Eli suddenly didn't want this moment to end. "Do you want to go for a walk?"

She smiled. "That would be nice. It's been quite a day, and going home to a peanut-butter-and-jelly sandwich doesn't hold a lot of appeal."

They made it out to the street, and five minutes later they were at a local park. This time of year, the greenery was in full swing, and Eli took a deep breath, knowing in a few months this would all be covered in snow. But knowing that didn't make him want to move to a warmer climate—it just made him appreciate Alaska's summer all the more. Just like he could enjoy these few moments with Georgia, knowing they wouldn't last.

"I'm so glad Edna is going to be okay," she said.

"I am too," he said, "and I'm hopeful that by trying to knock down the inflammation so quickly the myocarditis won't cause any lasting damage to her heart muscle."

There was no need to adjust his pace for her—Georgia had a long stride and had always moved with grace and speed. And he had to admit it felt good just to walk alongside her again. There would have been no doing this when she'd first arrived back at Anchorage Memorial. He'd even doubted they could work at the hospital together. All that had changed. And it seemed that maybe they could as well, although the jury was still out on that.

"How soon will you know?"

He stiffened before realizing she was referring to Edna and not his thoughts. "We should see a change in a couple of days if things go the way I hope they will."

They entered a curved stand of evergreens, where several benches were laid out. Georgia dropped onto the nearest one and breathed deeply. "I missed this place. I used to come here all the time after work. On days I was alone, I'd run. It was freeing."

He sat down beside her. He remembered coming here with her more times than he cared to remember. They'd often stopped at this very same place to talk. About work. About the weather. And about them.

"And I remember skiing in this park in the winter on our days off," he said.

Knicker Park had groomed trails in an area of woods for all levels of skiers. Or flat areas where you could cross-country ski. They had often come here just to burn off some of the stress of the day.

"That was fun," Georgia said. "So was meeting up with that moose when we were headed to the chalet for Hot Chocolate Night when the hospital hosted their annual Christmas party there."

He chuckled. "I was busy judging the distance between it and us and wondering if I should just scoop you up and run for the chalet."

She turned toward him with a laugh. "I didn't know that. Thankfully it decided we weren't very interesting and turned and went the other way."

The mirth on her face drew him in. They'd had a lot of good times together. He'd never quite understood where it all had gone wrong. One day they'd been fine and the next, she'd been gone.

It had always been hard to resist her. And right now, as the breeze made strands of dark hair sift across her face, it was no different.

He lifted a hand to touch her cheek, easing away some dark tresses that dared to blow into her eyes. She was still smiling, lips parted slightly. She was so beautiful. And when she looked at him like this, it made a dark heat generate in his gut.

This time was no different. Her head tilted slightly as if judging the angle of his, and before he realized what was happening, he leaned over and touched his mouth to hers.

CHAPTER SIX

HER WHOLE BEING IGNITED.

It was as if Georgia had been waiting for this moment ever since she'd come back to Anchorage. Eli's mouth was just as firm and warm as she remembered. Just as sexy. And it sent a bolt of electricity through her body that morphed into some equally dangerous reactions. All of which were addictive.

And she wanted more.

Her hands went behind his neck and tangled in his hair as if afraid he might try to pull away before she'd gotten her fill of him. Not that she'd ever been able to do that. No matter how many times they'd kissed, no matter how many times they'd made love, she still craved him.

Despite the three years she'd spent away on Kodiak, that was one thing that evidently hadn't changed.

She pulled him closer, relishing the feel

of his tongue pressing for entrance—an entrance she granted far too quickly. And yet it wasn't quick enough, judging from the way her senses were lighting torches. Torches that paved the way for an ecstasy she could only remember.

His tongue filled her mouth, and she couldn't stop the quiet moan at how good it felt for him to do this. And when the crook of his elbow went around her waist and hauled her against him with a bump, her arms twined around his neck. How utterly heady it was to be wanted by a man like this. A man who was so different from the others she'd dated during her younger years. A man so different from her father. She was never afraid when she was with him. Not even when he'd proposed.

The scar on her left wrist seemed to burn for a second, and it startled her, making her break free. She sucked down a quick breath, unsure of what had just happened. Or why.

Eli's low voice came through. "Are you okay?"

"Yes." But she wasn't sure. She untwined her arms and slid a few inches away. Far enough that she could feel her thoughts coming back to taunt her, telling her they knew she couldn't resist letting things go further than they should. Telling her she never should have come here.

"I'm sorry, Georgia. I'm not sure why I did that."

She shook her head and gripped his hand between hers for a few seconds before letting go. Her emotions were still scattered, and she wasn't sure she was going to get them back under control. "It wasn't just you. It's this place. It's always been this place. There's something magical about it. Almost as if it traps you in a fairytale the moment you come through the gates."

"I know." He shut his eyes. "But fairytales aren't real. And they don't always come true."

A slice of pain went through her. He was right—she knew he was. Things had not changed on her end, and unless he'd changed drastically in the last three years, they'd not changed on his end either, especially since he'd gotten married while she'd been gone. It might not have lasted, but that didn't mean that he wasn't still after the same things in life that he'd been after back then: marriage and a family. And who could blame him?

"Maybe I shouldn't ask, but just in case I run into her, is your ex still at the hospital?" She hadn't seen her or even heard anyone talk about her, but that didn't mean Georgia wouldn't ever have a child come through the ER and find it necessary to call in a pediatrician. And she and Lainey had had a pretty drama-free relationship, although there'd been a moment or two when Georgia had thought she'd caught the other woman looking at Eli in a way that had made her pause. Had the woman had a crush on him even while Georgia and the cardiologist had been dating?

"How did you know…" Eli pulled in a visible breath. "Of course. William."

"He didn't tell me everything you did, but he also didn't want it to come as a huge shock if I found out you'd gotten married a year after I left."

Eli seemed to stiffen. "It was hard after you left, and Lainey…well, she was there for me."

"I bet she was."

"What's that supposed to mean?"

God, she was making an even bigger mess out of this than she had that kiss that they'd just shared.

She touched his hand again. "I'm sorry. It doesn't mean anything. I'm sorry it didn't work out. I—I wanted you to be happy."

"Thanks. It just wasn't meant to work out, evidently. And to answer your question, no, she's not at the hospital anymore. She's in the Aleutians with her current husband."

Her current husband. Poor Eli. That had to have been hard. And he didn't deserve it. Just like he hadn't deserved what she'd done to him by turning down his proposal and leaving town.

She suddenly realized how her abrupt change of attitude had probably hurt him back then. But she hadn't been able to find the words to explain how utterly terrifying the thought of being chained to someone in marriage was. It was irrational, like a phobia that wasn't based on real experience. Except hers was. It was based on how her mom's entire identity had been subsumed by her dad, her existence only important insofar as it had served his wants and needs. It had taken her mom years to be able to think for herself. And once she had, there'd been no going back. Her mom wasn't risking her independence again. For anyone.

And as much as Georgia might've wanted to deny it, some of that had rubbed off on her. That fear of being engulfed by a partner. Eli's earlier choice of words about not wanting to make her feel less than had hit the nail on the head. While he hadn't made her feel that, there was a fear of that happening…with anyone, not just Eli.

"So what do we do about what just happened? Chalk it up to the park—our history here?" he asked.

"I think that's exactly what happened. And I think we were both happy that Edna's case didn't look as hopeless as it might have," she said. "So maybe this time we should just cut ourselves some slack and agree that it can't happen again."

"Cut ourselves some slack, eh? That concept is a little foreign to me, but I'll try."

She couldn't stop the spurt of laughter because he was right. She'd always had to remind him to do that, to not be so hard on himself, and it seemed that was something else that hadn't changed. "You can do it. I have faith in you."

And she did. Despite everything that had happened between them, Eli was one of the good ones. She'd never seen him do anything out of spite or even anger. So if she hadn't been able to allow herself to deepen her relationship with him, it didn't bode well for any other relationship she might have in the future. She would never meet another Eli. Not in this lifetime, and probably not in the next either.

He stood to his feet and held out his hand. She shook her head, softening it with a smile, and stood under her own power. Not because his offer was insulting, but because she was afraid if he touched her, she might pull him down for another kiss…or three or four. And that wouldn't be good. At all.

"So I'll see you at work tomorrow? I think I'm going to walk a little more," she said.

"I'll see you there. Be careful." He didn't offer to go with her, but then again, she had not asked him to, hoping he'd get the hint and not try to walk with her back to the hospital.

"I will. I'm not going far, and I doubt I'll see a moose this close to the park's entrance."

Georgia started off, giving him a little wave as she moved in the opposite direction of the exit. As soon as he was out of sight she would turn around and head back. She just needed some time to clear her head and try to figure out exactly what had happened here.

And to figure out how to avoid it ever happening again. Step one: never visit this park again with him. Step two: she had no idea. But hopefully she would come up with a game plan that made sure she was invulnerable to his charms. Or anything else the universe might throw at her. What was it they said? The best defense was a good offense. Which meant she needed to be proactive when it came to Eli Jacobsen. Proactive as hell about making sure she didn't find herself in a situation where she might be tempted to do or say anything that might lead to more kissing. Or worse.

Eli spent the next few days trying to figure out exactly what had happened at the park. Had he initiated that kiss, or had she? He still didn't know. And while it had been shocking to have her ask about Lainey, it had brought home the fact that he'd had two failed relationships and didn't want to risk a third. So that kiss could not happen again.

He actually hadn't seen Georgia since then. She'd been up to see Edna—the woman had gushed about how much she loved the ER doc and had made her into almost a superhero who had single handedly saved her life. He had to admit, she wasn't wrong. Georgia had put her butt on the line and risked having a complaint lodged by Ronny Mueller. Although, at this point, Eli couldn't see that happening, since it was obvious that the other doctor had made the wrong choice when recommending Edna be discharged with a change of meds.

Speaking of Mueller, Eli hadn't seen him either, even when he'd been called down to the ER by one of the other doctors who worked there. Unfortunately none of those patients had been the one that Georgia had told him about when she'd first come back to Anchorage Memorial, and he'd been actively looking for that name to come up. It hadn't. He could only hope that her symptoms had either died down or she'd sought the advice of another doctor.

Maybe Mueller had left for his vacation a week earlier than planned. That wouldn't be such a bad thing.

Shaking off those thoughts, he headed on his morning rounds, his first visit being Edna. The steroids seemed to be working. Edna's breathing had eased, and while she still needed oxygen, an MRI this morning showed less inflammation in the myocardium than the previous scan.

Knocking on the door, he entered and smiled when he saw that Edna was actually sitting in the recliner while Artie lounged on the bed.

"I just couldn't stay lying down any longer," she said. "My butt hurt."

"Hurt how?" Pressure sores were always a worry when patients were in one spot for too long, but according to her chart, Edna had been shifted every two hours just like protocol dictated, and when he glanced at it again, there was no mention of anything that would indicate the beginnings of a bed sore.

"It's nothing. I was just tired of lying down."

"But there's no deep pain anywhere?"

Edna laughed. "You mean like my son? He's been hovering over me ever since he got here. He went for a coffee, so he's out of my hair for a while. He didn't want me to move from the bed to the chair, even though the nurses gave the okay yesterday."

Eli smiled but tracked back to what she'd said about pain. "I just want to make sure you're not getting a pressure sore."

"Oh." Her face cleared. "No. I had one of those ages ago when I had pneumonia. It was not fun. No, this pain is nothing like when that started. The weird thing was when that sore was at its worst, it no longer hurt."

That was because pressure sores destroyed the nerves as they worsened, so patients often had no idea how bad things were until some-one actually looked at the area.

"You're still getting bed baths?"

"Yes. Because no one will clear me for an actual shower."

He walked over and laid a hand on her shoulder. "Remember what I said about need-ing to rest? This is part of the not-so-fun part of that. But you really do need to take it easy in order to let your heart muscle heal." When a look of horror came across her face, he was quick to add, "That doesn't mean it'll be months before you can shower. We just want to take it slow and easy."

He made a note in her chart to have the nurse look for signs of a pressure wound when Edna was bathed next. Just in case.

"Okay."

"Did Dr. Sumter come by today?"

Artie hopped off the bed.

"Yes, she just left a few minutes ago," Edna said. "She was actually the one who suggested Weston go for coffee. She could see how wor-ried he was and how frustrated I was getting. She made sure I made it from the bed to the chair without a problem."

Of course she had. But he was glad that someone had been there for that first solo transfer. "And your breathing was okay with the exertion?"

"I'm still on this tube stuff, but yes, it was okay. How much longer will I need oxygen?"

"Until your levels are within normal limits without the supplemental oxygen. They're getting closer. We've already weaned you down from one hundred percent oxygen to seventy-five."

Artie spoke up. "I'm only asking because Edna has been pestering me to—any idea when we can fly home?"

"I'm hoping by the end of the week, when we finish the steroids. I've been keeping your cardiologist apprised of your progress, and once we set up a discharge date, he's offered to clear a spot in his appointments so that you can go straight from the airport to his office just to make sure the flight wasn't too much of a strain on you. You can't walk through the terminal, though—you'll need to be wheeled to the gate."

He had to admit he was going to miss having her as a patient. She was funny, and yet she didn't dismiss his suggestions, even when she might not like them.

Her husband smiled. "Edna's already talking about coming back to visit. She likes what she can see of Anchorage from the window of her hospital room."

"Yes. I want to see a moose."

Eli's brows went up. "They're not quite as romantic as they might seem." He thought back to that day in the park with Georgia and how it had brought back memories of their times there. That moose encounter had been one of several. Fortunately none of them had resulted in an animal charging them.

One of the nurses popped her head in. "We have an air ambulance with two patients touching down from Dutch Harbor. ETA for the squad to get here is about ten minutes."

Dutch Harbor was part of Unalaska in the Aleutians, and air ambulances—when weather conditions permitted—carried patients to an airstrip near Anchorage Memorial. "Cardiac involvement?"

Eli had treated fishermen from the island from time to time who complained of chest pain or who were actively having a heart attack, but it wasn't an everyday occurrence. Usually the ER staff met the patient at the door and did the preliminary triage before calling in a specialist.

"From what I understand a young adult tried to jump from a rooftop onto a trampoline and missed, hitting his head on the side," the nurse said. "He's been unconscious since it happened. And when his father arrived on the scene and saw what had happened, he started having severe chest pains. They asked if you could meet the ER doctor out there since they're short-staffed today. Mueller is out sick."

Ah, so the man hadn't left for vacation early after all. "Okay, I'll head down there."

He made sure Edna was comfortable before he left, asking her to have one of the nurses there when she decided to get back on the bed. Artie was staying in the room with his wife. He wasn't sure where the son was staying, but probably in one of the local hotels. Despite what Edna had said, it sounded like their son was a caring individual and would make sure the couple got any help they needed once they arrived back in Florida.

Eli took the elevator down to the ground floor and headed to the ER, which was busy. Not good if they were short-staffed.

Georgia met him in the hallway. "Thanks for coming. There are just two doctors in, and we're backed up already this morning. The medevac team evidently had a hairy ride to Anchorage, since the winds on the island weren't cooperating."

He heard the sound of a siren, and she visibly tensed. "I hope to hell that's the EMT transport from the airstrip rather than another emergency on top of everything."

Two minutes later the truck pulled up and the driver jumped out. "We've got Ted Parker, the possible heart-attack victim here. The medevac team said he passed out in transit despite the treatment and his EKG is all over the place."

Georgia frowned. "And the other patient?"

"They should be here any minute. They're having to be careful. Suspected spinal involvement in addition to the head injury."

"Got it," she said.

They unloaded the first patient, and Eli noted the bluish tint to the man's lips and nails. Something was definitely going on. His heart wasn't getting enough oxygenated blood to his body. "Let's get him inside."

"Good luck," Georgia said. "I'll wait here for the head-injury patient."

"Sounds good." Eli could only hope things were better than they sounded.

They got the patient into an exam room first so he could at least get a handle on what was happening. "How long's he been like this?" he asked the EMT.

"About five hours. The air-ambulance team said he got progressively worse in the three hours the team was in the air. They were having to work on both the patients at once."

Not the best-case scenario, but sometimes it was unavoidable.

"Okay—thanks."

Thankfully the ER was ready for them, and they got the patient shifted from the EMT's gurney to the one in the room, and Lauren and another nurse came in to hook up leads for an EKG. As soon as he saw the tracing he knew they were going to have to act fast if they hoped to save the man. "I want to get him up to Imaging. Can you call ahead and let them know I have a patient who needs a CT coronary angiogram?"

"I'll call." Lauren left the room, and he helped the other nurse take off the leads so they could move him.

An orderly came in, and he and Eli rushed the patient to the elevator. The sooner they got him upstairs the better.

The patient was still unconscious, and so they got him into the imaging department, where they were just finishing up with another patient. But it didn't take long, and soon they had the dye injected and Ted put into the CT machine.

Eli went into the control room, where a tech sat, to watch as the images appeared on the screen, and within five minutes, he saw the issue. There was a major blockage in two of the arteries that supplied the heart. Almost completely shut. Damn.

"Too big for catheterization?" the tech asked.

"It's right on the border. I want to try that first, though, before jumping to bypass surgery. Let's get him out."

While he waited for them to finish up, he called to see if there was a surgical suite available, wondering how Georgia's patient was faring. But there was no time to call and ask.

Fortunately there was a room available. If the stent didn't work, they were going to have to crack his chest and do a bypass. He called up to the cardiac unit and asked them to send some of the team in for the catheterization and to call for the rest to be on standby in case a more invasive procedure was needed.

Within twenty minutes, Ted was in the operating room and Eli had made the cut in the groin that would give him access to the vessel needed. Watching the screen, he slowly advanced the catheter, making his way to the arteries that supplied the heart. When he got to the first blockage, his jaw tightened. It was going to be tricky. But it was worth a try.

If all went well, they would put the stent in place and then use a balloon to expand it, pushing the blockage against the walls of the artery.

The hard part was getting the stent through the blockage. Calculating the best placement, he worked the catheter through, got it into place and then put the stent where it needed to be.

"Okay, inflating the balloon now." He watched the monitor until the stent was fully expanded. As soon as it was in place, he saw an immediate increase in blood flow through the vessel to the heart. A sense of relief filled him. He'd done the hardest vessel first because if Ted was going to need a bypass, he'd rather know now than wait until the second stent was ready to go and realize it wasn't going to work.

"We got it," he said. "Now let's go on to the second one."

It took less time to place a stent into the second blocked vessel, and that one was also a success. He withdrew the catheter, noting the cyanosis was already markedly improved.

"Let's call that a success. Thanks, everyone." He talked to one of the surgical nurses. "Liz, can you call and let them know I won't need the bypass team right now? Thanks." He handed the catheter to one of the other nurses. "I'm going to close the entry site, and then we'll get him up to Cardiac ICU for observation."

Hopefully during that time Ted would wake up. Seeing his child seriously injured had certainly precipitated the cardiac crisis, but it had also probably saved his life. If he hadn't been treated now, in a few short months he might have had a full-blown heart attack and not made it to Anchorage in time to survive.

Eli hoped the son was faring well too, although he didn't know the state of the young man's injuries.

By the time Ted was settled into a room in the cardiac-intensive-care area, he was beginning to come to. An ultrasound had shown that blood flow had been returned to the heart, although they still weren't certain how much tissue damage there'd been. A blood test had shown elevated enzymes that indicated some damage. Whether that damage was temporary or permanent was still to be seen.

Eli leaned over the bed. "Ted, can you hear me?"

The man nodded, his eyes coming up to meet Eli's. Grizzled cheeks spoke of a life lived outside in the elements, and he thought he remembered hearing that the man was a fisherman. That occupation in Alaska was not without dangers of its own, and he could see how the stress of a dangerous job might have contributed to Ted's heart condition. And he might have to make some major life changes in the future.

"M-My son?" The words were weak, but Eli understood what he was asking.

"I haven't heard anything yet, but he's getting the best care possible."

"Substance..." The rest of the words were too low to hear, but a flicker of alarm went through him.

"Does he have a substance-abuse history?"

The man nodded. "Heroin. In treatment."

Eli wasn't sure if the medevac team had this information or not, but it was important. "Okay, I'll make sure his doctors know that. Hang tight here while I make a phone call."

He bypassed the desk and took a chance that

Georgia's cell-phone number was the same as it had been three years ago. He frowned at the fact that the number was still saved in his own phone, but it was more due to neglect of keeping up with those types of things than due to any hope of reconciling with her.

She answered on the second ring. "Hello?"

"Are you still treating the medevac patient?"

"He's getting an MRI right now. It doesn't look good, though. Possible brain bleed, and there's no pain response in any of his limbs."

"Fractured cervical vertebrae?"

"Yes. C3."

"Damn."

"That's what I said when I saw it."

He sighed. "I hate to add to your worries, but his father just woke up and says the son is in treatment for a heroin addiction."

"Oh, no. Is he off it?"

"Not sure. The dad is still too weak to communicate clearly. Can you call Dutch Harbor and see if you can find out any information? It might make a difference if he's going to go through withdrawals. And jumping off a roof… It could be either a stupid stunt, or he could have been high at the time. I'm guessing he wasn't in a residential treatment center, or it's doubtful he would have been home."

"Agreed," Georgia said. "I'll see if I can find out. I'm not even sure if the kid's mom is in the picture."

"Yeah, I didn't get any information on that either. I'm going to guess not, since we haven't heard from any relatives," he said.

"Okay, I'll let you know."

Georgia sounded exhausted. If the busy ER was any indication, she was probably run off her feet, and although a neuro team had likely taken over the son's case, Eli knew her well enough to know that she would follow the young man's progress as much as she could.

"Hey," he said, trying to catch her before she hung up.

"Yes?"

"Are you okay?"

"I think so. He's just so damn young. Just nineteen. There's no guarantee he'll even pull through, and if he does and if his cord has been severed or compromised, he may be paralyzed for the rest of his life. How's his father doing?"

"I just got done placing two stents. He's stable, but the jury is still out on how much permanent damage his heart has sustained."

"Okay. Keep me updated."

"I will. You too on the son."

"Will do. Bye, Eli."

She disconnected, and he stood there for a few minutes holding the phone, realizing how ridiculous it was to have thought they could work in the same hospital without ever interacting with each other. If she'd been in another department, say Oncology, it would've probably worked. But the ER was the heart of the hospital—it pulled patients through its doors and then pumped them out to whichever department was necessary to continue treatment. So of course he was going to see or hear from her on a regular basis.

But they'd just communicated without any problem. That was a good sign, right? They'd been professional, and there hadn't been any hint of anything happening under the surface. At least on her end. On his, however, the second he'd heard her voice his nerves had taken a hit and his heart rate had sped up. He'd been in no hurry to end the call. She'd done it instead. Not good. But if they remained at this level, he could handle it. As long as she didn't show any romantic interest in him.

You mean like that kiss?

That has been an anomaly. Nothing like

that had happened since then. And it probably never would again. If Lainey suddenly came back to the hospital, there'd be no chance of them getting back together. So if Eli just treated Georgia like he would Lainey there would be no problems.

Except she wasn't Lainey, and from what he'd seen, she hadn't left him for another man. She'd left because she didn't want to commit to marriage or to him for the long term. And while that should have provided him with some level of comfort, it never really had.

Well, it was doing no good to stand here trying to figure out how things were going to go between them in the future. He needed to get back to his patients—Ted and the rest of them, including Edna. But it looked like Ted was going to make it anyway. That was something worth celebrating. Then he would hope that Ted's son would do better than expected with his injuries. And that his mind could stop dwelling on Georgia every time they interacted. Because down that path lay nothing good.

CHAPTER SEVEN

BRANDON TEETERED ON a precipice. His condition was so precarious that no one talked in terms of the future. Everything right now was measured in minute-by-minute increments. Twenty-four hours after being admitted, his team had still been dealing with multiple concerns. The most troubling was bleeding on the brain. If it continued, they'd have to make a hard decision about whether to remove a section of his skull to relieve the pressure and hope that it would soon let up. Because the bleed was deep in the brain and surgery was not looking promising.

Another complication was that the fractured vertebra was pressing on the spinal cord. If it had been severed, survival would have been less likely as breathing would have been compromised. But even without being completely severed, if they couldn't knock down the swelling and inflammation, he was still in danger of paralysis below the neck, and if it got bad enough, he might need to remain on a ventilator for the rest of his life.

As for his heroin addiction, they were trying to balance his meds so that he didn't go into full-blown relapse. And right now, he was in a medically induced coma to try to manage all of that. The question was whether or not he would ever wake up or regain normal brain function after such a traumatic injury.

Time would tell. But it was hard knowing that if Brandon died, his dad would be alone in the world. Ted's wife had died of cancer when his son had been just entering his teens. It had evidently played a part in his drug addiction.

Georgia couldn't imagine the heartache of Ted losing both his wife and his only child. It was incomprehensible.

Her shift had already ended for the day, but for some reason she found herself hanging around, just in case they needed her.

For what? What could she do that the best specialists in Alaska couldn't do?

She took out her butterfly charm and twirled it between her fingers as if it held some kind of healing power. But in reality it didn't. It was just a reminder of something that didn't seem to matter at the moment.

How much more heartache would it be for Ted if his son's brain function was severely damaged? He might not simply be confined to a wheelchair but unable to feed himself or communicate. What if Ted had to care for him for the rest of his life? And having a heart condition himself, she could imagine him worrying about what would happen to Brandon if he had a heart attack and died.

She hadn't heard from Eli since yesterday's phone call, and it bothered her that she kind of hoped he would call her today as well, if only to give her an update on Ted or Edna.

But she'd seen Edna earlier today, and she was doing well. In fact they were getting ready to fly out of Alaska the day after tomorrow. Ted had made it through his surgery, and Eli had said he expected the man to make a full recovery. So what would he even be calling her about? Just to say hi? To say he missed her?

Gah! The one thing she did not want to do was start hoping for that. Doing so would put her back on a road that had dead-ended three years ago. She already knew what was at the end of it, so why was she still hoping to talk to him?

She had no idea. It had to be the good memories of the past that were leaving her so unsettled. If she could focus on how their relationship had ended, it would be better for both of them. But how did you do that when your emotions were craving just the opposite? She had played that kiss in Knicker Park over and over in her head, trying to remember every nuance and sensation, fearful that it would just disappear if she didn't. Especially since she didn't think it would ever happen again. She was pretty sure Eli was a whole lot stronger than she was in that area and wouldn't be caught off guard a second time.

Georgia could only hope that she could do the same. Because she'd come to the conclusion that *she'd* initiated that kiss. She remembered staring at his mouth and tilting her head to an angle that…that what? Would give her the most satisfaction?

Yes.

And if she did it once, wasn't she more likely to do it again? Or at least want to?

Because she did want to, even now. No matter how high the price. How pitiful did that make her?

It had to be her libido. She hadn't been in a relationship for the last three years, so her body was craving something that her mind said she shouldn't have. At least not with this man. So was she planning on being celibate the rest of her life?

No. But as hard as it was to have sex without the relationship part, surely there were ways around that. If she knew that Eli wouldn't expect more down the line, it could even be with him. After all, Georgia knew they were compatible in that area. More than compatible. In fact she'd never had better.

In her heart of hearts, though, she knew it wouldn't be fair. Knew that he would want the deeper emotional intimacy that went along with the physical part. And she couldn't give that to him.

Her cell phone chirped, and her whole body went tight with anticipation. She dropped the butterfly back into her shirt before looking at her phone. Then she frowned. It wasn't Eli. It was one of the hospital's internal numbers.

Probably just calling to give her an update on Brandon.

"Hello?"

"Hi. Dr. Sumter? This is Terri Kinsley. I'm one of the nurses in the neuro ward."

Ah, so it was an update. "How's our guy doing?"

There was a pause. A heavy one, and she suddenly knew what was going to be at the end of that pause. Her heart went still for a moment.

"I'm sorry, but Brandon passed away a few minutes ago. Despite decompression surgery, we weren't able to get the bleeding in his brain to abate. Between that and the continued swelling..." There was another pause. "And his spinal cord was severely compromised. It was doubtful he would ever have regained use of his body below his shoulders, and—"

"I get it. He's gone. Thank you for letting me know." She ended the call knowing she'd been abrupt, but the sudden rush of tears made her fearful she'd start sobbing over the phone, something that was neither professional nor helpful to anyone. It wouldn't change the outcome. Nothing would.

Sitting on a bench in the hospital courtyard, she swiped at the moisture on her face, irritated at herself while mourning the news Ted would soon be hearing. It wasn't fair. Neither was life, though. Her mom had not deserved what her husband had put her through. Neither had Georgia. And yet it had happened.

She bowed her head, cupping her hands on either side of her temples to hide her sudden emotional meltdown from anyone passing by. She'd hoped he would make it. Had hoped Ted, at least, would get a happy ending. At nineteen, Brandon had had his whole life ahead of him. He could have beaten his addiction, had a wife, kids, provided hope for his dad, who'd already lived through one loss. Now Ted had another to contend with.

She squeezed her eyes shut, trying to get control of herself. But another tear plopped onto the ground, despite doing her best to hold them in.

A hand laid on her shoulder, and she stiffened. God. She didn't want someone she didn't know asking her what was wrong.

"Georgia…"

She recognized that deep voice, could picture the face that went along with it.

Glancing up, knowing her chin was wobbling and her eyes were not only wet but probably red as well. "He died, Eli. Brandon died."

"I know. I just got the call and came to find you." He dropped down onto the bench beside her. "I hoped he'd make it too." He tipped her face up and used his thumb to dry the area under one of her eyes.

"I—I just can't believe it. I knew it was a long shot, knew in my heart he probably wouldn't make it." She shook her head. "But I wanted it for him. So much. Isn't that crazy? I didn't even know him. Never talked to him. I don't even know what color his eyes were."

"Not crazy at all." He looked at her face, and there was a long pause. "Are you working tomorrow?"

"No. I have the day off." She sucked down a breath. "God. I am such a mess, and I'm not sure why."

"Listen, I have a cabin about forty-five minutes outside of Anchorage. Do you want to go there just to get your mind off of things for a while? I can give you the keys, and you can—"

"I don't think I can go there alone. Not when all I'll be able to think about is—"

"How about if I go with you? If you think that would help. Or do you just want to go home?"

She didn't. It was probably one of the reasons she'd hung around the hospital. She did her best to remain objective when she did her job, but every once in a while a patient came along and got under her skin. Both Edna and Brandon had done that.

"No, I don't want to go home either. The cabin sounds nice, if you can spare the time away." She wasn't even sure why she was agreeing to him going with her. But she really didn't want to be alone.

"I don't have anything pressing right now. Ted is out of danger, although he hasn't been told about his son yet. That can happen later tomorrow, when he's stronger."

Tears welled up all over again. "That poor man. First his wife and now his son."

"I know. But all we can do is be there for him. Or call someone who can."

"Yes." She glanced at him. "Are you sure about the cabin?"

"I am. We can leave right from here if you want."

Her shoulders relaxed. "Thank you. I have a change of clothes in my locker. Let me just grab them, then I'll be ready."

Eli stood and held out his hand, and unlike in the park, this time she accepted his offer. "I'll let the staff in my unit know where I'll be and meet you in the parking lot. If you get there before me, it's a white SUV."

As opposed to the sleek black sports car he'd had back when she'd known him? A heavier vehicle made a lot more sense for

Alaska anyway, although she'd liked the other vehicle. Especially the time they'd parked on a plot of land he owned and…

No. Don't think about that.

Trying not to dwell on Brandon, or things in the past that she couldn't change, Georgia headed toward the staff lounge and pulled out the tote from her locker that held an extra set of clothes. She was feeling shaky and slightly sick with the turmoil of emotions she'd been dealing with after hearing the news of Brandon's passing. Maybe the cabin would give her a chance to reset and push away the deep sense of melancholy that was cloaking her like one of those weighted blankets. Except those blankets were meant to instill the user with a sense of security and warmth, and this felt nothing like that. This felt suffocating, like she couldn't draw a deep breath. So she'd let Eli take her to the cabin, where her mind could dwell on things other than death. Or loss. Or things that nothing could change.

Eli waited beside his car. He wasn't sure why he'd offered to let Georgia go to his cabin. Or worse, why he'd offered to go there with her. He had no explanation other than the fact that she seemed so broken over the fact that Ted's son had died. Eli was sad too, but at least his patient had made it, and that helped balance any sorrow he might have felt. Taking her to the Valley with him probably wasn't his smartest move, but what else could he do? It wasn't like they were going there for some kind of liaison that would end with them in bed.

It was just a neutral place where Georgia could decompress a little bit and try to get her emotions back under control. Everyone who worked in a hospital setting found themselves needing that from time to time. Not everyone owned a cabin, but almost everyone had a place they could go to to pull themselves together—even if that place was a just a spot in their own home.

Eli could at least give Georgia a spot like that. He knew how much she hated to lose control in a public place. She liked to be fully in command of her emotions at all times. But sometimes that just wasn't possible. It wasn't that Eli lost his cool in public, but he had his office, where he could go when he needed privacy at work. Like when Georgia had left him holding that little ring box. The ring had been as much an impulse buy as the proposal that went with it had been.

He hadn't saved the ring. Hadn't wanted anything that reminded him of what had happened, so he'd talked to Steve, who had offered to find a couple in need who were getting married. He had and had gifted the ring to them. This couple was in the Big Brothers Big Sisters program, something Steve had gotten involved with after he and his wife had been ready to retire from their foster parent duties—which had been pretty soon after Eli had graduated from college. He'd often joked with his mentor that fostering him had made Steve realize how tough that gig was. But Steve had been kind, just as he'd always been, and said that he'd wanted to go out on a high note.

Georgia came out of the building carrying some kind of flowery canvas bag. It must've contained the change of clothes she'd talked about. Seeing her made him wonder again what the hell he thought he was doing. Going to a cabin where it was just going to be the two of them? That seemed like behavior of a crazy man.

But he had to remember this was to help Georgia. And because she hadn't wanted to go alone. He hadn't had the heart to sit there in silence, especially after seeing how hard Brandon's death had been on her.

He opened the back door for her and let her put her things in. "Do you mind if we stop by the grocery store for supplies? The cabin is off-grid, so I don't keep the refrigerator running when I'm not there." Fortunately, they'd had several days of sunlight, so his solar panels should have charged his batteries fully.

"It's fine."

"Anything in particular you want?"

"Coffee?"

"You got it." While he was there he could pick up a couple of steaks and some things for breakfast in the morning. He didn't imagine they'd spend more than just a day there, and he had an extra cooler up there that he could use to transport any leftovers back to his place.

Eli pulled into the big local grocery store. "I'll just be a minute…unless you want to come in."

She glanced at him through the big sunglasses she'd put on. He wasn't sure if they were because she was still weepy or because of the sun. But whatever it was, he couldn't read her expression and found that he didn't like that. "Do you mind if I just wait in the car?"

"Not at all. See you in a few minutes."

Getting out of the car, he headed up to the store.

Fifteen minutes later, he had everything, including some hot chocolate. Even though it was warm outside, the nights could be cool, and she might want to sit out by the fire pit once it was dark enough—not that they had many hours when the sun wasn't in the sky this time of year. But Georgia had always loved hot chocolate the few times they'd gone camping.

After he got back into his vehicle, they headed down the road.

"Where is your cabin?" she asked. Her head was tilted back against the headrest, and she looked exhausted. Or lost. Or maybe a little bit of both.

Something in his heart shifted. A protective instinct that he had always had with her, for some reason. She was a perfectly capable, strong human being, but every once in a while he'd spotted a fragility in her that he hadn't quite understood. Kind of like one he'd spotted today. The one that had made him offer her the use of his cabin.

"It's actually in Mat-Su Valley. You were there once. The land didn't have anything built on it at the time."

Her head jerked toward him. "You mean...?"

"I'm afraid so. Do you still want to go?" He remembered every second of making love to her there when he'd still had his other car. It was part of the reason he'd gotten rid of the thing.

"There's a cabin there now, right?"

He wasn't sure what that had to do with anything. "Yes. Steve helped build it."

"You guys built it? On your own?" That seemed to shift her away from what had happened there.

He nodded. "We got some help setting up the solar array, but other than that, yeah." He smiled. "It's not very fancy, so don't get your hopes up. It has a well, so there's running water, but it's powered by solar panels." It only had one bedroom, but he did have a couch that converted into a bed, so he'd figured he'd sleep there.

"It sounds wonderful. That land was beautiful, from what I remember of it." She paused and then continued. "How is Steve anyway?"

Georgia already knew his whole life story, so she knew that he'd been raised in foster homes and that Steve and his wife had been his saving grace.

"He's doing good. Still doing the Big Brothers Big Sisters stuff."

Eli wanted to ask how Georgia's mom was, but she'd always been a pretty private person, which he hadn't found odd when they'd been dating for some reason. He knew where she'd grown up and that her mom was basically her only living relative, but as far as how her life had been as a child, he'd been pretty much in the dark, other than the fact that her mother had raised her single-handedly.

"That's wonderful. Does he ever go and stay in the cabin?"

"Every once in a while. But he's more of a homebody, so he'd rather just stay at home with his wife, unless it's their anniversary or something."

"But you evidently go there?"

"Whenever I can. I love it out there. It's peaceful and quiet and on ten acres, so there aren't other cabins right on top of mine."

"It sounds like heaven."

It hadn't been right after Georgia had left him, and the memory of them making love out there had almost spoiled the property for him. But he'd decided to build the cabin anyway, thinking he could sell it if he still felt the same way in a year or two. Surprisingly, the building process had somehow numbed the pain. Brandon had turned to drugs, while Eli had turned to sweat and hard work. Two months later, his cabin had been born. A place where he could go lick his wounds in private, and hell if he hadn't needed that during the six months that had followed his breakup. He'd only surfaced to go to work and do what needed to get done. Sometimes he still did that: escaped whatever hard case he'd been working on, using the cabin as a place of solace and time to recharge his emotional batteries. It worked, and he doubted he would ever get rid of the place now.

"I like it. It gives me time to be alone."

As soon as he said the words he regretted them, hoping that Georgia didn't take them to mean that he was sorry he'd offered the place to her.

Instead she nodded. "I completely get that. It's why I've always liked Knicker Park. I used to jog there. I may start up again. I saw that the hospital has a 5K coming up. That might give me a goal to look forward to."

The last summer she'd been here, they'd run that race together, even though running had never really been his thing. It had been a lot of fun, though, when she'd been there with him. And afterward at his place… He closed his mind off to thoughts about what had come after, knowing it wasn't a smart idea to reminisce about things like making love when that was not what they were headed there to do. It would only make the stay awkward and difficult, especially if she guessed the reasons behind his discomfort.

He didn't want to make her feel uncomfortable. Besides, this wasn't about him. It was about Georgia, and he'd do well to keep his mind on that fact and not let it retrace avenues that were best left in the past.

"The park is the perfect place to do that." Eli hoped she wouldn't ask him to join her in training for the race. Because he couldn't do it. Not anymore.

Even the thought of spending time with her at the cabin, when there wasn't any work to keep his mind occupied, was seeming more and more like the worst choice ever. But there was no going back and undoing it. Trying to get out of it at this point in time would mean driving all the way back to the hospital and letting her drive herself to the cabin. At this point he doubted she would even go, and from the look of her, she needed this time. And he wasn't going to do anything to take that away from her. Even if it meant he was going to have to deal with a little discomfort.

CHAPTER EIGHT

GEORGIA GOT OUT of the car, a sense of amazement coming to her. When they'd traversed the track leading to the cabin, she hadn't been able to see much besides a rutted path that made her wonder if they would even make it. And there was absolutely nowhere to turn around. They'd have to back up, and with the brush scrubbing the sides of the vehicle, she didn't quite think that was going to happen. What happened if the conditions were so bad that he got halfway and got stuck?

No wonder he'd traded his sports car in for an SUV. And honestly, this vehicle seemed to suit him much better.

When she glanced at Eli, he was staring at her. Was her hair sticking up at an odd angle or something? "What?"

"Just waiting for you to say something. You held on to that armrest with a death grip the whole way down the driveway."

"It didn't make you nervous?"

"What? My driving?"

She laughed. "No, of course not. There's just not much room for error down that driveway. What if we'd gotten stuck?"

"There hasn't been much rain and the vehicle has four-wheel drive, so that wasn't likely. But I agree that I need to do a little work clearing it back again. I just haven't had time this year. Sorry you came?"

She looked again at the cabin, and some of the horror and sorrow of today seemed to melt away. "Oh, no. Not at all. This is beautiful."

When he'd said it was a cabin, she'd pictured some kind of stick-built structure with siding. Kind of like a smaller version of a house...or more of a shed-type building. But this was nothing like that. The outside walls were made of hewn logs that interlocked on the corners, kind of like those building blocks she'd had as a kid. In contrast to the cabin, the door was painted a sleek turquoise color that made it stand out from the natural color of the logs, something she couldn't imagine Eli choosing for himself.

She glanced at him. "I like your door color. It's so...you."

He grinned, the sideways tilt making him

look boyish and carefree, like the man she'd once known. Her heart swelled. She was glad he had someplace like this he could run to in hard times.

"The color was actually Julia's—Steve's wife's—idea. It used to be brown, but she said in the dark it was hard to find the entrance and asked if I'd mind if they painted it. The next time I came up, it was that bluish-green color. It's not something that I would have chosen, but I actually do like it now that I'm used to it. And the door is definitely easier to find in the dark."

"It fits the place perfectly. It looks like something out of a magazine, actually."

Nestled in a little clearing, there were still big pine trees around the cabin, but the spot wasn't crammed full of brush and other plants. It looked like the place had been here for hundreds of years. She vaguely remembered the land itself from the time he'd brought her here, and it had been wild and beautiful, even then. But now? It was something most people only dreamed of having.

"You said you built this place?" she said.

This time when he looked at her, there was a darker air to his face, his smile fading away. "Yes. A couple of years ago."

A couple. As in two? Or…three? Had he built this in the aftermath of their breakup? Somehow the thought of that made her incredibly sad. But then again, at least he'd put whatever emotions he'd had about what had happened into something he'd be able to use over and over again. And what had she done? Bought a silly butterfly charm.

The piece of jewelry seemed to burn against her skin, and she put her hand there for a second. It hadn't seemed silly at the time, though, and it had served as a reminder of why she'd done what she had. And Eli had gotten married again a year later, so he hadn't been that torn up, evidently. He'd moved on and been happy again. At least for a while.

Georgia was beginning to wonder if she ever had. Because right now, it seemed as if she were stuck in some kind of twilight that was neither night nor day. A kind of limbo where the days seemed to run together. Kind of like the deep summer of Alaska, when the dividing line between days wasn't always clear. People talked about the difference between night and day, but sometimes the contrast wasn't as stark as that. Sometimes it was just a kind of gray that had little to delineate it from what came before or after.

Like a brown door on a brown cabin? Where one element seemed to merge with whatever was around it? Was that what her life had become?

She realized Eli was waiting for some kind of response. So she blurted out the first thing she could think of. "I bet Lainey loved this cabin."

Oh, God. What a thing for her to have said. Especially since Eli and his wife were no longer together.

"She actually wasn't the biggest fan of the place."

Her eyes widened. "What? Why?"

He shrugged, face hardening. "I'm sure she had her reasons."

Georgia couldn't imagine anyone not falling in love with a place like this. "Okay, tell the truth. Did she decide she wasn't a fan before the turquoise door or after?" She wasn't sure if her attempt to lighten the moment was in the best taste, so she added, "I'm sorry, Eli. I shouldn't have brought her up."

"It's okay. Our relationship has been over for a while. I'm surprised William told you about it at all, actually."

"He didn't tell me much. Only that you'd gotten married and to whom." And Georgia could remember that moment like it had been branded onto her heart. Lainey. The woman who'd seemed to lick her lips whenever she'd looked at Eli. That was probably an exaggeration, but still...

A little part of her had imagined that he'd go on like she had, with no significant other anywhere in the picture. The fact that he'd fallen in love again—and with Lainey of all people—had been a cut that had never quite healed. She kept telling herself that she wanted him to be happy, but...had she really? Or had she wanted him to suffer after the breakup like she'd suffered. Except she'd been the cause of all that angst, not him.

"I see." He opened the rear passenger door of the car and got her tote bag out as well as the few bags of groceries he'd purchased. "Are you ready to go in?"

"I am." Anything to derail her thoughts and to change the topic of conversation. Which, of course, she'd been the one to initiate. Again.

She spotted a fire ring a short distance from the cabin along with a covered three-sided building that housed an impressive supply of firewood. "Do you think we could have a fire? Or is this not the right time of year?"

"It should be fine," he said. "While it's

dried up some, we did have some rain a couple of weeks ago. Plus I have the firepit set up with a large area of sand around it, so there's not much chance of the fire spreading. We can even cook our dinner over it if that sounds good to you."

"It sounds amazing. Thank you for bringing me here," she said. "I think I really needed this. I'm not sure why Brandon's death hit me so hard—maybe it was just because of all the loss that Ted has been through. I hope he's going to be okay."

"Me too. I hope he'll be able to channel his grief into something that will help him in the future."

Like this cabin? Was that what Eli had done—channeled his grief over their breakup into something that would help him in the future? He'd confirmed that he hadn't built it after his marriage had broken up, because he'd said his ex-wife hadn't been a fan of the cabin. So it meant he'd built it sometime between his and Georgia's breakup and his marriage to Lainey. But whenever it was, she was glad he had it, hoped he would keep this place for the rest of his life. She knew if she had something similar, she would use it as often as she could. And it sounded like he did.

"I hope he will too. Even if Brandon had survived he probably wouldn't have been the same," she said.

"No. He probably wouldn't have been the same."

Something about the way Eli said that made her glance over at him, but he'd already started walking toward the door, leaving her no choice but to follow him.

If she thought the outside of the cabin was beautiful, it was no match for the inside. Most of the walls that she could see had drywall covering them, except for the one where a wood stove sat. That one showcased the cabin's natural logs. And it fit, looking rustic and homey. There weren't a lot of windows in the main living area, but the ones the cabin did have boasted spectacular views. In the middle of the space was a worn leather couch, its overstuffed cushions looking inviting and comfortable.

"Do you come here in the winter?" she asked.

"When the roads are passable, I do," he said. "I've started taking my vacations in the winter and just holing up in the cabin for a couple of weeks. It's peaceful. And as you know the hospital can have a frenetic pace that wears you down to the bone."

"It does, but the opposite is true as well. When the pace lags too much, it can be just as hard to deal with."

The facility she'd worked at on Kodiak had been smaller, and there'd been times when she'd sat around for hours at a time with nothing to do but help straighten up the waiting room. But then she hadn't had a lot of people like Brandon come through the doors either. Oh, there'd still been drugs there, just like in most places on the planet, but smaller populations still meant fewer people came through the doors of the ER—other than with minor complaints like runny noses or sore throats. It was one of the reasons she'd come back to Anchorage.

"The hospital you worked at wasn't busy?" Eli asked.

"It could be. But we weren't the largest clinic on the island, so the most serious cases were automatically sent to main hospital."

"That makes sense."

He set the groceries on a wooden counter in the kitchen on the far side of the room, which, despite its small size, had a full-sized fridge. That made sense if, like he said, he came here for weeks at a time. It looked like the cabin was one large room. Which made her wonder what the sleeping arrangements were going to be. A tingle went through her that she tried to stop in its tracks. He hadn't brought her here for that. Besides, she'd noticed two doors. Surely one of those led to an actual bedroom. Or maybe there were two.

"What's behind those doors?" she asked.

"I'll show you." Crossing the space and leaving her to follow him, he opened the first door.

Ah, yes, so there was a bedroom. And what a bedroom it was. The bed had massive posts on each of its corners, much like the logs that made up the walls of the rooms. "Did you make that bed?"

"I did. I had some leftover wood and needed something to do with them, so…"

The headboard that connected the logs was a live-edged plank, the irregular border along the top giving it a sense of movement that no straight board could replicate. "I love it." She glanced at the walls, which were devoid of pictures or artwork, but there was a large rug covering much of the plank flooring. "Hmm…no moose antlers anywhere? I thought that was a requirement of every cabin in the woods."

"I've never been much of a hunter, although I do enjoy the moose or elk jerky I can buy at the local mom-and-pop grocery," he said. "We'll look at the trail camera and see what kind of visitors we've had, if you want."

"I'd love that." Her mind put to ease about the sleeping arrangements, since she assumed she would bunk on the couch, she asked about the other door.

"It's a bathroom," he said.

"So no outhouse?"

He laughed. "Actually, there is one. I tend to use it during the winter, when I can get to it."

"What? Why on earth would you do that?" The idea of tramping out to another building in the snow didn't sound like very much fun.

"It's actually not that bad. Remember I told you the cabin is off-grid? That means I'm not hooked up to the city's sewage system, and getting the land surveyed for a septic tank seemed like a lot of trouble. So the toilet in the cabin is a composting one."

"Interesting." She wasn't sure if she was telling the truth or not about that, but she was game to try it. And the cabin didn't smell like anything except for the warm scent of wood, so it must've worked pretty well.

He opened the door to the bathroom, and it was actually surprising. The countertop was polished wood, like in the kitchen, but there were faucets and a pretty blue bowl that served as a vessel sink. There was also a shower made up of shiny corrugated metal walls and ceiling. A rainfall shower head hung in the middle of it.

"I thought you didn't have plumbing," she said.

"I have plumbing, just not a septic tank. I have a well and an on-demand water heater that runs off a propane tank—that tank also supplies the gas stovetop and oven. The water used for showering or washing dishes goes to a gray water–holding area that I use to water the plants, if and when needed."

Even the toilet looked clean and modern. Not a simple bench with a hole cut in it, like she'd been expecting. "You'll have to explain how to use that."

"It's not very hard, and it's a pretty efficient setup."

"I'll take your word on that," she said.

Maybe that was what his ex hadn't liked about the cabin, because everything else was perfect. More perfect than Georgia could have pictured, actually. And to get to spend time here? With this man? She couldn't imagine anything that sounded more like paradise than that.

She swallowed. Yes, it did sound like paradise. But it was a paradise that she'd been banished from due to her own neuroses. So she had no right to expect to be able to reenter it. Ever. Because when it came down to it, nothing had changed. She was still terrified of being tied down to another human being. Her fingers started to go up to her charm before she realized he was looking at her expectantly. Maybe he thought she'd be disgusted or hate the cabin like his ex-wife evidently had.

She moved toward him and touched his arm. "I love this place. It's beautiful. And peaceful. I can't imagine anything more perfect."

Except to maybe share that bed in the other room with him. Or that inviting-looking shower.

Neither of those things were an option.

"Thanks. I'm glad you like it." They left the bathroom. "Are you hungry?"

She tried to remember the last time she'd eaten. Lunch? Definitely not dinner. She glanced at her watch. Seven o'clock. Way past the time she normally ate. "I am, actually."

"Good. Let me get a fire started outside, and we'll cook our steaks out there. I have potatoes too that we can fry or wrap in foil and throw in the fire to bake."

Her mouth watered. "Baked sounds delicious and a lot less work."

"I like the way you think."

Did he? He might have at one time, but he definitely hadn't liked it on the day he'd proposed to her. She never wanted to go through anything like that again.

"Can I help with something?" she asked.

"No, I need to chop a little bit of wood, but that shouldn't take long," he said. "There are some books in those shelves over there, if you want to sit and relax for a while."

She was still feeling pretty antsy, so the thought of sitting on the couch stewing in her thoughts didn't sound like a whole lot of fun. "Do you mind if I look around outside instead?"

"Not at all—help yourself. There are a few trails if you want to explore a bit. As long as you come back the way you go, you should be fine."

She didn't really want to go on a hike by

herself, so she opted to walk around the clearing area while he gathered an armful of wood from his neatly stacked pile. A few minutes later, she settled in one of the rocking chairs on the wide porch and tucked her feet underneath her and let her eyes close.

A sharp sound made them pop back open just in time to see Eli wield an axe and bring it down on a piece of wood, splitting it on the first try. He was still wearing the red polo shirt that he'd had on at the hospital, and the sleeves showed off his biceps to perfection as he chopped another log into pieces. There was something mouthwateringly attractive about a man chopping firewood. Or maybe it was just because it was Eli, but she couldn't take her eyes off him. He was gorgeous and talented and strong. And he'd once been hers.

How stupid had she been?

Pretty damned stupid. But better to end things when they had than to get married and find out that she couldn't bear having to report her comings and goings to someone or tell him how she spent her money. To let someone control her the way her dad had controlled her mom.

Eli would not have tried to control you.

She knew that. But no matter how many times she tried to convince herself that he was nothing like her father, the fear remained. A shadowy phantom that never really showed its face. At least not in a way that she could fight it. It was just a wisp of gray that materialized and then drifted away, just like the smoke from the campfire that Eli would soon be building. And she hated it. Hated that she'd allowed that fear to destroy the best thing that had ever happened to her. But better that than to destroy Eli by forcing him to live in a nightmare of her own making. And she wouldn't do that, no matter how tempted she might be to give them another chance.

A few minutes later he had the fire going and had the potatoes bundled into aluminum-foil jackets. He then seasoned the steaks and put them into a wire basket that he set on a grate over the fire. The scents were out of this world. She wandered closer and dropped into one of the Adirondack chairs that sat near the fire. "That smells so good."

"Hungry?" he asked, sending her a smile from where he knelt by the firepit.

"Yes." The one word came out, and she realized it encompassed so many things. Things that had nothing to do with the food he was cooking. She'd been hungry for the sight of him for the last three years. Hungry to have him look at her with something other than the shock and anger that she remembered from their last night together. Hungry for his touch, for his mouth on hers. To feel him deep inside of her.

She swallowed as the sense of melancholy threatened to wash away the peace she'd felt when she'd walked around the cabin. She'd messed up so many things. And there was nothing she could—or would—do about them. It was better just to let them go and try to find a way to be friends with Eli. Surely that would be enough.

Except she wasn't sure it would be. Because leaving had never erased the feelings she had for him. It was why she'd never gone back to casual dating after their split.

She loved the man. With all of her heart. She just couldn't trust herself to be with him. Or with anyone. She closed her eyes and tried to process the emotions that had risen from the dead after being buried deep in her subconscious for the last three years.

"Are you okay?"

His words made her glance over at him again. "Yes. Just enjoying the outdoors."

A lie. Just like so many she'd told him over the years when her fears would rear their ugly head.

This time when he looked at her, there was a dark look on his face that said he didn't believe her. "What's wrong, Georgia? Is it Brandon?"

"No." She stared at him for several seconds before simply saying, "I've missed you."

There was no sound other than the sizzling of the steaks for what seemed like an eternity.

"Don't." His voice was low and gruff and filled with something she didn't understand. But it told her he didn't mean what he'd just said.

She went over and knelt down next to him. "I'm sorry. But you wanted the truth."

Did he? Eli didn't remember using those words. But now they were lodged like a spike in his gut. A spike he didn't dare pull out without risking a lot more damage.

She missed him? Somehow he'd pictured her as moving back to Kodiak, feeling a relief similar to the one he'd felt when his divorce from Lainey had been finalized. He'd pictured her going about her life with a sense of laissez-faire, while he'd been up here splitting logs and trying to forget that Georgia Sumter had ever darkened his doorway.

But he wasn't quite sure he'd ever succeeded, no matter how much sweat and backbreaking work he'd poured into this place.

Eli hesitated for a second, trying to figure out whether to brush off her words or to dive headfirst into them.

He picked up his silicone mitts and took the wire basket containing the steaks out of the fire and stood.

"W-What are you doing?"

"Come on. We're going inside."

Georgia rose to her feet. "But the potatoes…"

"Do you really want to worry about potatoes right now?"

"No." There was a breathiness to her voice that said she'd just realized exactly what he was saying. Knew exactly what was in his thoughts.

Madness. That was what was in them. Pure and utter madness. But he couldn't get her words out of his head. They were playing over and over again.

I missed you.

Hell, he'd missed her too. Only he'd thought he'd finally gotten rid of all of that when he'd gotten together with Lainey. But maybe it had still been there. Maybe Lainey had sensed it and had been driven into his best friend's arms because of it. He knew he'd withheld part of himself from her. At the time he'd told himself that he wasn't, that he'd given Lainey all he had left to give, but looking back, it wasn't true.

He set the wire basket on a table outside the door, dropping the mitts beside it, uncaring that the juices from the meat might puddle all over everything. Right now he didn't care anything about the food, despite the fact that a half hour earlier they had both claimed to be hungry.

Pushing the front door open with his back he held out both hands to her and willed her to take them. This was the moment of truth. Either she'd backtrack and say he'd misunderstood her meaning or she'd take his hands and let him pull her inside the cabin.

The second her fingers slid across his palms, a deep shudder went through him. He tugged her against his chest, backed with her into the living room.

"Shut the door, Georgia."

When she went to pull free to do so, though, he tightened his grip, afraid if he let go she'd somehow slip from his grasp.

Maybe she sensed that because she mimicked what he'd just done a few seconds earlier. She put her back against the door, walking him with her until the barrier shut with an audible click.

He moved in, crowding her against the wooden surface. But she didn't complain when he let go of her and pressed his palms on either side of her, bracketing her with his arms.

She leaned her head against the wood behind her and looked up at him, lips parting. God. Just like when he'd kissed her less than a week ago. That now seemed like forever.

Too long.

His head lowered, and his mouth met hers with a hard groan that spoke of how much he had missed her too. He lost himself in the sensations that came roaring back to greet him.

Home.

It was as if he'd come home after a long, long absence. And it felt so good. So damned good to be able to touch her without feeling guilty. She'd asked him to do this. It was in the way she returned his kiss, her lips moving beneath his. It was in the way her arms twined around his neck and she raised up on tiptoe to get closer to him.

Eli couldn't resist her. He never could. His body was already strung so tight, he didn't think he was going to be able to make it to the finish line. But he would give it his best shot. Reaching down, he hauled her up against that tightness, relishing the way her legs wrapped around his hips…the way her body seemed to cradle his against her.

He pressed into her, wishing their clothes were gone, wishing he could take her right against the door she'd admired when they'd first arrived.

Had that been only an hour ago? Surely not.

But right now, he didn't want to leave this place. Wanted to stay here with her for weeks, making love to her on every available surface until they were both spent. But they didn't have weeks. They only had a matter of hours.

Don't think about that. She's here. That's enough. At least for right now.

So he kissed her again before spinning her away from the door and carrying her toward the bedroom. How crazy was it that a few hours ago he'd been thinking about sleeping conditions?

He was thinking about them again, but in a completely different way. In a way that had anticipation singing through his veins. Normally his body waited until after it had gotten its satisfaction before wondering when it would happen again. But it was greedy and was already planning scenarios in every available spot on the planet. Including his office. Including his apartment. Including his heart.

No. Not that.

Taking those words off the table, he went through the bedroom door and dropped her onto the mattress. She gave a laughing screech and bounced a time or two. He gave himself a few seconds to stop and look at her, hardly able to believe Georgia was at his cabin and that he would soon be making love to her in it.

This place had been built *because* of her, not *for* her, and yet here she was. And unlike his ex, she seemed to love everything about the place.

Even him?

It was a question he didn't dare ask. Didn't want to ask because he wasn't sure it would make any difference. He'd been broken when she'd walked away from him, and it had taken a long time for him to put himself back together. But he had. And he vowed he would never give anyone that kind of power over him ever again.

Stop thinking, Eli. Start doing...

He was going to live in the moment and not worry about tomorrow or any other day.

Leaning over Georgia, he kissed her thoroughly, taking his time before reluctantly pulling away so he could undress her.

And God in heaven, how he wanted to undress her.

He tugged her up so that she was sitting, and then he pulled her gauzy white blouse over her head, noting a smudge of dirt from the fire on her left sleeve. She didn't seem too worried about dirt. She had a necklace with a butterfly that dangled almost to her breasts. He'd never noticed it before, but then again, she probably kept it out of sight when working since it could get hung up on equipment and the hospital wasn't a big fan of wearing jewelry while on the job anyway.

He kissed her again as he reached behind her to undo the clasp on her bra, then eased it away. It was amazing how he still had every line and curve of her body memorized as if it hadn't been years since he'd seen it. Right down to the freckle she had on the side of her right breast. It was still there. Unable to stop himself, he bent over to lick it. Georgia's response was immediate. She arched up to meet his touch, and he couldn't stop himself from wrapping his arms under her back to keep her in place, moving his attention to her nipple and suckling deeply. She moaned, and it sent him into the stratosphere.

Suddenly, he couldn't get her clothes off fast enough, even though she kicked her shoes off and then lifted her hips to help him get her pants off. Then her panties, which he peeled down in slow motion, relishing the final reveal and what it meant.

For a second he stood over her, staring down. A brief moment of disbelief made him wonder if he was sleeping and this was all a dream. But then her eyes opened and she looked at him with those gorgeous green eyes, and he knew this was real. Very, very real.

She was here. In the flesh.

Still sitting, she tugged his shirt free from his pants and pushed it up his torso, the slide of her fingers along his skin making his flesh come alive. He ached. Needed more. So much more.

He yanked the shirt the rest of the way off and tossed it to the side, where it landed on top of hers. Just like the way he would soon land on top of Georgia.

His pants and briefs were soon discarded as well, and she held her arms out to him, wordlessly asking him to come down and meet her. But he had something he needed to do first, even though it was the last thing he wanted to think about right now.

He went over to the nightstand next to the bed and retrieved a packet from the drawer and ripped it open with his teeth. She looked at him, and her eyes widened. Had she totally forgotten about it? Or did she not want him to use it?

He had to. Couldn't take the chance that whatever was happening between them could fall apart all over again. So he sheathed himself and then walked over to the bed. He nudged her knees apart and slid his palms up her thighs.

She squirmed at his touch. "Eli…"

"Shh, I just want to enjoy you." When he got to the juncture of her thighs, he covered her with the heel of his hand, pressing it against the spot that he knew was the most sensitive.

Georgia made a noise deep in her throat as he released the pressure and then repeated the act in a rhythmic motion that mimicked what he wanted to do to her. Her hips lifted to meet his every touch, and the sight of it was sexy in a way that his brain couldn't put into words. But she was his. At least for tonight.

Then she was swiping his hand away. "Eli, I need you. Please…"

Her meaning was clear, and he was more than ready to oblige her. He lowered himself onto her as her fingers found him…encircled his length. The light pressure was almost his undoing. Then she was guiding him to her, and the second he was in position, he plunged deep, the moist heat at the heart of her making him see white for a second or two. Then he was kissing her, moving over her. The scrape of his skin against hers was something erotic…was something he'd almost forgotten but not quite. It was stored in his muscle memory, along with everything she liked. Everything that drove her wild. Everything that made her want him all the more.

And that made him want *her* all the more.

She was incredible…the way she fit against him…the way her hands slid over him.

He couldn't stop himself. He moved faster, his fingers going to her hips and gripping them to bring her along with him. The momentum built like a piece of music that was scaling up for something big. Something that would drive it over the top.

Suddenly Georgia's feet were on the bed and she was pushing her hips into him with a force that drove him deeper...deeper. And then he felt it. Her body went off, the crazy motions ending in the deep rhythmic pulses that demanded something of him with every contraction—every time it gripped and released him. Until he couldn't resist the lure of it any longer.

He fell over the edge into insanity. He thrust into her over and over again, pouring himself into her until there was nothing left. But he didn't want it to stop. Not yet. So he kept moving, kept trying to preserve this moment for all time.

Then the frantic movements slowed, easing him back to Earth as he pressed his lips to her neck and breathed her scent, letting it waft into his very cells.

Her arms went up his back, hugging him close. It made him feel wanted in a way he hadn't felt in a very long time. He pressed his cheek to hers as he caught his breath and just let himself be held.

Three words swirled around in his head

before landing on his tongue. He had to grit his teeth together to keep them from spilling out over them both. Now was not the time. And it had to be just sentimental notions from their past that had somehow melded with the present.

So he would hold on to the words. Until he was sure. Until he knew that it was about today and not about what they'd once had together. Until he was sure that the words were reciprocated. Because one thing he didn't want was for that last awful event of their relationship to happen all over again.

CHAPTER NINE

THE NEXT MORNING brought new wonders as Georgia sat astride him, loving the feel of him with each pump of her hips. She'd woken up before him and had rained tiny kisses over his neck. What she'd thought had been a dream had turned out to be very, very real. The slight ache of her body that had greeted her along with the light flooding through the windows had said last night had really happened.

His arm had anchored her to him, her body molding to his nakedness. Waking up next to him had been a study in decadence. And she loved it. Loved him.

"God, Georgia…"

His husky words made her smile. She couldn't remember the last time she'd felt so fulfilled. So content to just…be.

There was no rush. No hurry.

He palmed her hips, not pushing her toward an invisible finish line but letting her continue her leisurely pace. Last night had been kind of a blur of need and want, and she was having trouble remembering exactly what had happened or how it had even started. This time she wanted to commit every second of her time with him to memory.

Her fingers slid up his firm abs, seeking out his flat nipples, and she strummed her thumbs over them, loving the way his breath huffed out as she did so. He cupped her nape, drawing her down to his mouth. Kissing her deeply, his tongue and teeth echoed what she was doing to him. But again, it wasn't rushed. It was slow and methodical, as if he, too, were relishing every second of their time together, as if he wanted it to go on forever.

So did she. And she wasn't quite sure how to make that happen.

But right now, she didn't want to ponder the future.

She just wanted to be with him.

She sat up again and touched a finger to his lips, outlining the firm curve, her eyes taking it in with a new sense of wonder.

The man was perfect. In every way. And he did it for her. He always had. Fast or slow. Hard or gentle. She'd always wanted whatever he'd been in the mood for back when they'd been a couple. But this time it was different. It wasn't that he'd always called the shots before. But this time it was as if he were deliberately letting her take the lead. And it gave her a newfound sense of power. And she found she loved it.

"What do you want, Georgia?"

She smiled down at him, seating herself fully onto him and then rising up again in slow increments that made her sigh with pleasure. "When I know I'll tell you."

Her words weren't just about sex, although she knew that was what he'd meant by his question. But she didn't know what she wanted. Not really. Not outside of these few precious hours that they'd spent together.

His hand reached up, and she felt a slight tug of something around her neck. She glanced down and saw he'd captured her butterfly charm and had it trapped between his fingers, gripping it tight.

Something about the sight made her blood run cold, and her movements faltered.

"This is pretty."

His words were low and rumbly. He was still holding it, and it was as if he were imprisoning more than just her charm. It was as if he was holding her too, although she knew that wasn't his intent. Still, a sense of claustrophobia began building in her chest. Within seconds it threatened to overwhelm her. The longer he held that charm, the more panicked she felt.

She couldn't stop herself from trying to yank it from his hand, but when she did the chain broke and the butterfly tumbled to the bed beside them and lay as still as death.

No one said anything for the next few beats. The only sound was of their breathing.

"Georgia?" He tried to touch her cheek, but she jerked away, climbing off of him and kneeling on the mattress. She stared at the butterfly, the broken gold chain still gripped in her palm.

"Georgia?" he said again. "What's going on?"

"I don't know. I—I just can't. I need to go home."

He sat up, still trying to look at her face. "I'll take you."

Oh, God, the thought of being trapped with him in the car for the next forty-five minutes was unbearable. Her face burned in humiliation over her reaction to him making a simple comment about her necklace. What would happen if a much bigger subject ever came up?

Coming here had been such a big mistake. "No, I can call someone to—"

"Take my car. Steve has been wanting to spend time at the cabin. I'll just have him come over, and he can take me back to the hospital. Just leave the car there."

"I don't know the way." She gathered the sheet around her naked form. In reality her words were about a lot more than just how to get back to Anchorage.

"Just take the track back to the road. Your GPS will get you back to the hospital from there. My keys are on the table in the kitchen." He paused, face inscrutable. "Call if you have any trouble."

A wild sense of hope came over her. He was giving her a way out—without making her feel crazy or ridiculous.

"A-Are you sure?" She did her best to ignore the fact that he was still lying naked on the bed. She'd taken the sheet for herself and the duvet was on the floor, so there was nothing left for him. Something about that seemed prophetic.

"I've never been more sure of anything in my life."

Georgia swallowed. Prophetic indeed. This was the end. She could hear it in his measured tones. In the calm, cool blue of his eyes. There wasn't a wave or a ripple of emotion within them. No, he hadn't made her feel crazy, but he was letting her know that there was no coming back from this. Not for them as a couple anyway.

It was for the best, right? It was what she was asking for.

She scrambled off the bed and gathered her clothes, taking them with her into the bathroom. She didn't bother showering—she could do that once she got home. Instead she pulled her clothing on piece by piece, glancing into the mirror as she zipped up her jeans. Her face stopped her short. Her hair was a hideous tangled mess and her mascara smudged from sleeping in it, but that wasn't what caught her attention. It was the pale unhappiness that she saw in her reflection. The raw pain that came with knowing she was about to leave the only man she'd ever dared to love. And he was done. Done with this trip. Done with spending time together.

Done with her.

She should've been relieved that this hadn't

been messier. That he'd let her off the hook basically unscathed.

Unscathed? No. She might not show it on the outside, but she was cut and bleeding on the inside, from wounds of her own making. Her fingers went to the rippled flesh on her wrist and rubbed it until it ached.

This scar might have been caused by her father, but the rest of them? Those were on her. And Georgia had no idea what to do about any of it. For right now, though, all she could do was run away from the situation. And she was so tired of running. So damn tired. So this was the last time for her as well. And she meant that with all of her heart.

She grabbed the keys off of the table and got into Eli's vehicle, pulling the seat forward so she could reach the pedals. Then she started the SUV and carefully made her way down the overgrown track, wincing as branches caught at the large vehicle, but it never hesitated. Not once. It was as if it knew what she needed.

When she got to the road, she stopped, laying her head on the steering wheel and allowing herself to cry in the silence for several minutes. Then she sat up and scrubbed the heels of her palms over her eyes and told herself to suck it up. She'd made her choice, and now she was going to have to live with it. Then, setting her GPS, she turned right like it told her to do and took the road that would lead her back to Anchorage. Back to a life she was no longer sure she wanted.

The drive seemed to take forever, but finally the hospital was in sight. Carefully pulling the big vehicle into the employee parking area, she saw her car. Someone was leaning against it. Her heart stopped for a second before she realized there was no way it could be Eli. She got closer and saw the person was William. She frowned. God! Had something happened to her mother? To Ted or Edna or one of her other patients?

There wasn't a spot right next to her car, so she had to park Eli's car a few spots over. Then she got out, grabbed her tote bag that she somehow remembered to get before leaving and left his keys under the floor mat like she told him she'd do. Then she hurried toward her friend.

She didn't waste time on pleasantries. "What's wrong?"

William's brows went up, and he pushed away from the car. "I could ask you the same question."

That puzzled her. There was no way he could know what had happened, other than the fact that she was driving Eli's vehicle. "What are you doing out here?"

He shook his head and came over and gave her a hug. "Eli called me and asked me to make sure you arrived safely."

"He told you?" Horror washed over her.

"He didn't say much other than telling me that you'd had to return to Anchorage and were driving his vehicle. Is everything okay with your mom?"

"Yes. It's..." She licked her lips as tears again rose to the surface and threatened to spill over, just like they had as she'd left the cabin. "Can I call you later? I—I just need to get home and do some thinking."

Draping an arm around her shoulders, he looked into her face. "Think long and hard, Georgia. Because I have a feeling that whatever decision you come to in the next several days, it will be one you're going to have to live with. Now, I have to get back to work. Call me."

"I will. Promise." She looked at her friend. "And William, thanks."

She watched him walk toward the entrance, then leaned her back against the car and shut her eyes. Yes, he was right. This decision was one she was going to have to live with. What William didn't know, though, was that it had already been made.

She reached up for her necklace and realized she'd left her charm on Eli's bed. The events of the last hour played through her mind like one of those video clips from a social media site. And that was all that was left. Her memories.

Because she had nothing else to show for it. Not even the butterfly charm that had brought her world crashing down around her.

Eli fingered the butterfly, turning it over and over with his fingers as Steve sat on the couch in his cabin. Something about this little charm had wrecked what had been happening between him and Georgia on that bed. In reality, he had only commented on it as a way to take his mind off what she was doing to him, kind of like that old joke that all men thought about baseball as a way to slow down their rush to sexual release.

"Do you want to talk about it?" Steve asked.

The question jerked him from his thoughts. "No."

His friend already knew the basics. That

he'd come here with Georgia and that she'd had to leave unexpectedly, so she'd taken his car. His friend hadn't asked why Eli hadn't driven her back himself, but he was sure Steve had worked some of it out for himself. William had been the same way. He hadn't asked why Georgia was driving his vehicle back to Anchorage alone. But the nurse had texted to say that she'd made it. And that was it. No insight into what had precipitated her suddenly needing to leave.

Except Eli knew what it was. He just didn't know what it meant. The charm that had caused such panic in her seemed to burn his fingers. And that was what it had been. Some kind of full-blown panic attack. She'd been fine. Until he'd touched her necklace and commented on it. Then it had been as if a switch had turned on in her face, and she hadn't been able to get away from him fast enough.

Had the butterfly been given to her by another man, and she felt guilty for being at the cabin with Eli? No, Georgia wouldn't cheat on someone. Besides, if there was someone else, then she'd left him behind. Just like she'd done with Eli three years ago. On Kodiak, more than likely.

But he didn't think that was it either. Her

reaction mirrored what had happened when he'd proposed to her three years ago. Her eyes had widened, and then the same frantic expression had crossed her face. It had ended in her taking off and then finally moving away from Anchorage less than a week later. His attempts to call or contact her had been met with silence. There'd never been any explanation other than the fact that she couldn't marry him.

Would she leave Anchorage again? If so, he didn't want to be there when that happened. He preferred to wait here in his cabin, where there was no chance of having to say any kind of goodbye. He'd already called and checked on Ted and Edna. Edna was actually leaving to catch her flight back to Florida today. He'd spoken with her on the phone. And although Ted was grieving the loss of his son, the stents had done the trick and he was recovering. A colleague of Eli's who was semiretired but who rotated through the hospital on days that he couldn't be there had agreed to work his shifts this week. It would give him time to think. And time for Georgia to leave the hospital—if history was going to repeat itself.

"Well, if you don't want to talk, let's go do something besides mope around the cabin."

"I'm not moping." But he was. He was sitting here feeling damned sorry for himself, and it was solving nothing. Whatever was going to happen was going to happen.

"Whatever you say. But I'm going to take one of your fishing poles and I'm going to head for the lake," Steve said. "We're eventually going to need something to eat."

Eli had thrown the partially cooked steak from the previous night far into the woods when he'd taken a walk to clear his head. He was lucky a bear hadn't come along and torn up his porch trying to get the meat out of the wire basket. He'd been stupid to leave it out.

Actually he'd been stupid about a lot of things.

But what was done was done.

"I'll come with you. And you're right." He gave his friend a smile that was devoid of mirth. "You always could tell when I was bullshitting you. But I really don't want to talk about what happened with her, okay? Not now. Maybe not ever."

"You don't have to talk about anything but the weather if that's what you want." Steve got up and slapped Eli on the back. "Besides, too much talking'll scare the fish away, eh?"

* * *

Eli hadn't come back to the hospital. Two days had passed, and there'd been no sign of him. Edna, who'd been discharged yesterday afternoon, had said that the surgeon had called her to wish her well on her trip.

Georgia hadn't gone up to his floor for fear of seeing him. In fact, she'd been hoping not to run into him anywhere at the hospital. But after talking to Edna, she finally did go up to check on Ted, and he seemed to be well on his way toward a physical recovery, even though he'd been shattered to hear that his son had died without regaining consciousness.

Georgia had thought through her options. She could run back to Kodiak like she'd done before, or she could stay and try to work through her problems. That didn't include getting back together with Eli. But could she work here at the hospital with him after what had happened? She wasn't sure. What she did know was that she was going to start training for the hospital's 5K race as if she were going to be here for it. It was just a couple of weeks away, so there wasn't a whole lot of time. But it would keep her mind off of things and hopefully help with the lethargy that had stolen over her ever since she'd walked out on Eli.

With her shift for the day done, she went to her locker and pulled out her running clothes. She'd go to the park and train a little before going home. To her empty studio apartment. Something that seemed sad and lonely all of a sudden.

It had touched her heart that despite the way she'd left Eli's cabin he had been concerned enough to contact William and ask him to check on her. Her friend had texted her a couple of times asking if she wanted to grab lunch together some time, even cornering her as she'd come out of an exam room yesterday. But she'd kept putting him off. She wanted to talk to William about all that had happened but needed a little time and space so that she wouldn't be a complete and utter wreck when she did decide to tell him.

Georgia got changed and scraped her hair back into a ponytail, shaking her head at the strands that wouldn't stay in place. She really should let it grow back out some. But when she'd left Anchorage three years ago, she'd wanted a new start, and chopping her hair off had been part of that transition. Only she'd stopped jogging and so hadn't needed to pull her hair back any longer. Until now. But she wasn't about to change her appearance again because doing that had made no difference the last time, and it would make no difference now. She'd missed Eli like crazy three years ago.

And she missed him now. She couldn't believe she'd voiced that truth to him as they'd sat by the fire. But it had seemed like the right thing to do. At least at the time. In reality, that was what had precipitated them making love in the first place.

Heading out to the park, she ran hard, a stitch forming in her side almost immediately...the result of her body not being prepared to deal with the sudden return to training.

Actually her body hadn't been ready for any of the other changes she'd thrown at it in the last couple of weeks either—like finding out Eli wasn't married any longer, sleeping with him and then leaving him behind all over again.

She kept running, and the cramp in her side grew despite her efforts to just run through it. She finally stopped and leaned over to catch her breath, bracing her hands on her knees until the pain lost some of its fire. She had no doubt that part of it was caused by stress. But that wasn't something she could control, although keeping everything bottled up inside wasn't helping her deal with the emotional devastation that littered her heart and mind. She was pretty sure that psychological pain was now manifesting itself in physical ways. Like the pain in her side.

Gripping the cramped area, she made her way over to a nearby bench and dropped onto it and waited for the sensation to leave. So much for training and hoping it would take her mind off things. It hadn't. It had just brought everything into sharp focus.

Twenty minutes later she could finally take a deep breath without it feeling like something was going to rip apart inside of her. That was funny because she was pretty sure something already had when she'd left Eli's cabin two days ago. What if he never came back? His SUV was still parked in the lot. Her eyes had automatically been drawn toward it whenever she'd arrived at the hospital and then again when she'd left.

Surely he wouldn't leave it there indefinitely? Maybe his friend Steve hadn't been able to come and he was stuck at the cabin with no transportation.

He had a cell phone. He could call her—or someone else—if he needed help or needed a ride back to Anchorage. He obviously had reception on his phone, since he'd been able to call William a few days ago.

But she felt guilty about even the thought of him having to call for a ride. She had no idea what to do. About any of it.

Georgia really wanted her charm back. But how could she look Eli in the face and ask for it? Maybe she could tell him to leave it at the information desk on the ground floor of the hospital. Or maybe William would have an idea.

She finally did what she had put off doing. She pulled her cell phone out of her back pocket and dialed William's number. When he answered, she took a deep breath and said, "I'm ready to talk. You tell me when and where you can meet me, and I'll be there."

"How about right now at the Bear Claw?"

"I'm out jogging right now at the park, but I'll head back to the hospital. I can shower there and be at the Bear Claw in, say, forty-five minutes?"

"Forty-five minutes it is. See you there."

* * *

Steve and Eli sat in camp chairs on the shore of the good-sized lake, their fishing lines in the water, poles propped up next to where they sat. So far, neither had said anything outside of talking about the latest sports figures. Eli had put the butterfly charm on a table in the dining area of the cabin. He would have to get it back to her somehow. If worse came to worst and she disappeared again, he could always give it to William, who could probably get it back to her.

"The girl you were here with was the one you used to date before Lainey?" Evidently Steve was done beating around the bush because he opened up the subject with a point-blank question.

"Yes, she was."

"You still care about her?"

He shrugged, shifting in his chair. "Does it matter?"

Steve fixed him with a look. "Maybe. Maybe not. But what you do from here might dictate what happens over the next several weeks."

Several weeks. He couldn't even fathom that much time passing without being able to see her.

"I still care. But she…" He dragged his hand through his hair. "I have no idea what she feels. But this is the second time that she's suddenly run out on me."

"Since she's been back in Anchorage?"

"No," he said. "The first time was when I proposed three years ago. And the second time was two days ago when I made a comment about a piece of jewelry she had on. She suddenly said she couldn't and that she needed to go home. I have no idea what even happened."

"So we'll go back to my previous question. You still care about her. I'll add something to that. Do you care enough to go ask her how she feels about you?"

"She'll just run again."

"Maybe," Steve said. "But maybe, like you, she's mulling things over in her head. Something spooked her, and I know you well enough to know you didn't hurt her or try to scare her. That butterfly you were fiddling with back in cabin might have triggered some kind of fear, though. What do you know about her past?"

"Nothing, really. I know her mom is still alive and divorced, although I've never met her. I know her dad is no longer in the picture, according to her."

"As in she's estranged from him?" Steve asked.

"I think so. I tried to ask about him one time, and she was pretty quick to cut me off."

Steve reeled his line in, checked his lure and then sent it sailing back out over the water where it landed with a small splash. "Did you ever stop to think that maybe she's reacting to something in her past—whether it's from her family or someone she dated? After all, you went through some hard times when you were a teenager."

What was his friend talking about? His parents' deaths? Or about the questionable foster homes he'd been in?

"Yes? And…?"

"Did any of that stuff color the way you perceive the world?"

Eli raised his brows. "You saw how I was when I first came to your house."

"I did. So that would be a yes." Steve shrugged. "Don't you think that this girl could be struggling with some junk from her past too? We all come with baggage, Eli. Even me. And it took you quite a while before you were willing to talk about any of it."

"What if she refuses to talk? Or if she somehow can't get past whatever it is?"

"Did Julia and I give up on you?"

"No, but I don't know why you didn't sometimes." Eli really didn't. He'd put them through the wringer for almost a year.

"Because you were worth fighting for." Steve picked up his fishing pole and began reeling in his line again. "I remember meeting Georgia back when you were dating the first time. She seemed like a pretty special girl. Not the kind who likes to play games with people's emotions."

"I didn't think she liked to either," Eli said. "And yet she walked away. Not once but twice now."

"But you don't know why. And until you do, you'll never know if her reasons for walking away are something you can work through together or not."

Maybe Steve was right. He'd tried to call Georgia the first time she'd left, but he hadn't been very persistent. In the end, he'd given up. Whether he should have gone to Kodiak and confronted her was something he'd never know. And yet she'd told him she'd missed him by the fire not three nights ago, and the deep longing in her voice had made him think they might have a second chance. She hadn't left after they'd made love that first time. And he was more and more positive she wouldn't have after the second time either if he hadn't noticed that charm.

"So you think I should go and ask her."

"I think you should go and ask her." Steve stood to his feet and set his pole on the ground.

"Where are you going?"

Steve smiled and looked at his watch. "Julia should be here in about five minutes."

"What? You called her?" he asked.

"No. But I told her if she didn't hear from me by noon, she should just plan on picking me up at one."

"What if it doesn't work out between me and Georgia?"

"Then call me. But only after you try your best to talk to her and come to some consensus about your future," Steve said. "If it doesn't go well, I'll bring a six pack and some food, and we can eat and drink until nothing matters anymore."

The sound of tires crunching on the track to his cabin sounded, and Steve grinned. "Sounds like she's a few minutes early, so I'll head up there."

When Eli picked up his own pole to go back up to the cabin with his friend, Steve stopped him. "Why don't you sit out here for a while and enjoy the quiet? I'll tell Julia you send your love. And I'll leave the keys to my car on the table. Just in case."

"Thanks, Steve. For the company and the talk. And you're right—she's worth it."

Steve clapped him on the back. "So are you, Eli. Don't you ever forget that."

With that his friend was gone, whistling a tune as he walked back toward the cabin, which was barely visible between the trees he had cleared last year. Steve had left his chair and his pole right where they were, which made Eli smile. It was okay, though—it would give him time to think through a game plan. He could either drive back to Anchorage this afternoon and try to see if Georgia was still in town or he could wait until tomorrow. Because this time he wasn't going to just try to call her. He was going to go see her, whether she was still at the hospital or had moved back to Kodiak. If things were going to end this time, he wanted them to end face-to-face. And he wanted to know why.

He couldn't force her to tell him. But he could ask. Something he hadn't done last time. Until then, he was going to sit here for a while and enjoy the lake. He picked up Steve's pole and cast the line back into the water and sat back in his chair, pulling his ball cap down over his eyes.

CHAPTER TEN

SHE WAS BEING FOLLOWED.

As soon as Georgia turned down the road that led to Eli's cabin a small white car had turned its signal on as well and crept up the track behind her. A shiver went through her. Was this a mistake? Maybe Eli had already left and gone back to Anchorage.

But his car had still been in the parking lot. Once she'd talked things through with William, she'd decided she'd been a bigger fool this time about Eli than she had been the last time. She owed it to him to tell him why she'd acted the way she had. Both this time and when she'd left for Kodiak three years ago.

He might laugh in her face or tell her to get lost, and she wouldn't blame him. She was still feeling shaky about coming out here and telling Eli about any of this. And yet from the moment she'd met William at the Bear Claw, she knew she had to come and at least try.

Her friend hadn't even needed to say a word because all of it had just come pouring out of Georgia's mouth in a stream of consciousness monologue that had left her breathless and aghast at the time she'd wasted.

Why had she never told Eli about her dad? It wasn't as if she'd expected him to look down on her for something she'd had no control over. But she hadn't felt strong enough back then. Was she any stronger now? She didn't know, but she at least owed him an explanation.

And if he was willing to let her back into his heart?

Oh, God, she didn't even dare hope that he would understand. That he would be willing to help her figure out a way to be together in a way that was acceptable to both of them.

But right now she was worried about being out in the middle of nowhere with a car staying right on her tail. Maybe it was Eli.

No. As far as she knew, he only had the SUV.

The cabin came into sight, and she saw a second car in the parking lot. She swallowed. Maybe he was having some kind of party. One she hadn't been invited to.

Could she blame him?

Maybe he was glad to have her out of his life.

He hadn't seemed glad three days ago. In fact, he'd seemed pretty stunned by her sudden change in attitude. Well, party or not, she was going to see if she could pull him aside and talk to him.

She stopped in front of the cabin, just as a man—who was definitely not Eli—came out onto the porch. This man looked vaguely familiar with his gray hair and slight build. She glanced to the side as the white car pulled up beside her. In the vehicle was a woman, who waved at her with a smile.

Julia! This time she had no problem identifying the occupant. And when she glanced back at the porch, she saw it was Steve, Eli's foster parent from his younger years. She'd had dinner a couple of times over at their house when she and Eli had been dating.

Another thought came to her. One that made her leap out of the car. Why would they both be here? Unless…

Not wasting time on pleasantries, she leaped from the car. "Is Eli okay? Has something happened?"

Steve came down the porch and met her. "He's okay. But he was pretty devastated when I got here."

Georgia closed her eyes. "That was my fault. I was stupid and took off without telling him what was wrong."

Julia grabbed her close in a hug. "I'm hoping that means you're here to do just that and not just to return his car."

"Yes, but…" She glanced at the door, which was still closed. No sign of anyone inside that cabin. "Where is he?"

Steve dropped a kiss onto his wife's cheek. "He's over at the lake fishing. I was going to leave my car here for him to get back to town with, but…"

"I'm hoping after I tell him what I came here to say that he'll be willing to spend the forty-five minutes trip back to Anchorage with me."

Steve laid a hand on her shoulder. "I rather think he'll be willing." He glanced at Julia. "That means I'll have to follow you back home. Or I could leave my car here to pick up later."

She gave her husband a slow smile. "Why don't you leave it here? I missed you and could use the company on the drive back."

"That works for me." He went back to the porch and picked up a small duffel bag and threw it into the back seat of Julia's car. "Like

I said, he's down by the lake." He pointed through a stand of trees. "You can't miss it."

She pulled in a deep breath. "Do you think he'll be willing to talk to me?"

"I'm pretty sure he's not going to let you walk out of here *without* that talk."

Julia gave her another hug. "Go to him. We look forward to hearing something good from your visit."

Promising she would do her best, she left her stuff in Eli's car and headed in the direction Steve had pointed, hoping she didn't run into a moose or bear on the way. Eli never had had a chance to show her that trail cam he'd set up on the property.

She'd never been so aware of the sounds of twigs crunching underfoot, of the sounds of leaves rustling in the breeze or the way the sun cast dappled patterns on the ground. Less than two minutes later, she saw two camp chairs and a man sitting in one of them.

Eli. At the sight of him, her eyes began to burn and her heart thumped a hundred miles an hour. What if Steve was wrong? What if Eli had washed his hands of her? She couldn't blame him. But God, she hoped he would at least listen to what she had to say.

She quietly walked in front of him to catch

his attention, only to find he had a cap pulled down over his face.

Was he asleep?

Going over to the second chair, she slowly lowered herself into it, trying to make as little sound as possible. If he was asleep, she couldn't think of anything she wanted more than time to just sit here and study him. Sit here and imagine that they were here as a couple and that he would wake up and smile at her. That he would walk her back to the cabin and make love to her without fearing she would walk out on him again.

Maybe that was what true freedom was. Being with someone without being afraid of what might happen. Of being secure enough in a relationship that you didn't have to walk on eggshells every time that person was around. She'd found that person. She hadn't realized it three years ago. But she realized it now. If only he would give her another chance.

"Forget something?" Eli popped his hat back onto his head and turned toward her. The smile that was on his face disappeared in an instant when he saw who it was. A cold shiver went over her. Maybe Steve was wrong. Because he sure didn't look happy to see her.

He sat there for a minute or two before reaching over to twirl a strand of her hair, looking into her face. "Did Steve call you?"

"No. Why would he have?"

Eli shook his head as if confused before letting go of her hair and leaning back in his chair. "Why are you here, then?"

She tried to find some eloquent way to explain herself and failed. She finally settled for something that was simple but true. "I wanted to explain why I left so abruptly the other day."

He nodded. "I was planning on heading back to Anchorage today to ask you that very question."

Again the thought that Steve had misjudged Eli wound through her head like the smoke from the fire the last time she was here, making everything cloudy and uncertain.

"You were?"

"I was. I was going to try to find you and ask what you're so afraid of." He touched her cheek, his touch warm and gentle, inviting her to tell him the truth.

She reached up and took his hand, twining her fingers through his. To her relief, he didn't pull away, just allowed her to keep his hand in her lap.

"It was my butterfly charm."

"I somehow worked out that much." He squeezed her fingers. "I just didn't understand what it meant. I still don't."

"I know. And if I hadn't been in such a blind panic, if I had stopped to take a breath or two, I might have realized that I wanted you to know."

"I'm listening now."

This time she didn't try to put the words together, she just started talking, hoping he could somehow untangle the jumbled thoughts and phrases.

"I bought that charm three years ago, right after we broke up. When you asked me to marry you, I panicked. Just like I did the other day. The butterfly was supposed to remind me that I could only be free to fly if I was on my own. Anything that tried to hold me down was immediately brushed aside, and I would take flight." She shrugged. "The funny thing was I never really felt free, even then."

"Does this have something to do with your childhood?"

She turned their hands over, exposing the scar on her wrist. "You're very astute. My dad was a controlling and jealous man. My mom couldn't do anything without telling him.

She couldn't work. Couldn't have friends. Couldn't spend money without accounting for every penny that left her purse."

Eli lifted her hand to his lips and kissed the scar. "Did *he* do that to you?"

The graveled tones and the look in his eyes was enough to make her hurry to explain. "Not directly. But he got mad at me one day and threw my piggy bank on the ground, smashing it to pieces. One of the shards flew up and cut me. My mom kicked him out, but as I grew up, I saw my friends in relationships along with the petty fights and jealousies that happened in those relationships. I decided that I would not be controlled by anyone ever again. Not my dad. Not my boyfriends. Not even someone I cared for more than anything."

She hoped he would understand she was talking about him.

"Why didn't you tell me?"

"I'm not sure. I guess I thought it wouldn't change the way I felt. That it wouldn't change my mind about relationships preventing me from being free."

"Do you still think that?"

She sighed. "I have to admit, I'm still scared. But I think I'm coming to realize that true freedom only comes when you can be vulnerable around someone without fear of being hurt or ridiculed and ignored."

"Oh, honey, I am so sorry that *anyone* made you feel that way," Eli said. "If I knew where he lived…"

"No. He's not worth it. I don't know where he is, and I don't want to know. The most horrible thing is realizing I've let what he did back then control me for the last thirty years. I still gave him power over me. But no more."

"I'm glad." He pulled free of her grip and cupped her chin, turning her face toward him. "So what does that mean for you from here on out?"

"I'm hoping you can be patient with me and give me another chance. I'm hoping you still feel something for me because I still love you," she said. "I never stopped. And if there's a chance for us, I'm hoping that someday you'll ask me to marry you again. It doesn't have to be right now. It doesn't have to be within the next year. Or even ten years. I just want to know we'll be together. With or without the piece of paper. If you still want that."

He leaned in and kissed her. A kiss that was bright and beautiful and full of hope. "Georgia, I've never stopped loving you either." He paused. "But ten years really doesn't work for me."

A sense of fear went through her. Was he saying he loved her but didn't want to be with her again? She couldn't blame him for not trusting her after what she'd put him through. When she thought of the time she'd wasted, she didn't think she could—

He smiled at her, and the crooked tilt of his lips erased every trace of fear. "If I get down on one knee, are you going to run?"

Did he mean, like, right now? She waited for the sense of panic to set in, but there was only a sense of peace. Of fulfillment. Of love.

"No, I'm not going to run. Not this time." The words came out in a whisper. She was so afraid that she was dreaming. That she would wake up and find nothing had changed. That Eli was still at the cabin and that she was in her little studio apartment, feeling for her butterfly charm every time something made her nervous.

"In that case…" He slid from his chair and knelt in front of her in on the pebbly ground. "I don't have a ring, but we can fix that later. Georgia Ann Sumter, will you marry me? I love you, and I promise never to hurt or ridicule or ignore you. I promise never to make you feel afraid. For all of our days."

He was using her words from earlier and promising never to make her feel the way her dad had. And she loved him for it. And most of all, she believed him. Believed he would let her fly high and that he would be right there soaring right along with her.

"I will, Eli. I will marry you. I love you."

With that he pulled her out of her chair and down beside him, rolling her on top of him and holding her tight against him. And there was no claustrophobia, no sense of being trapped. They were together and in love. And there was no greater freedom than that.

Suddenly there was a splashing sound, and a sense of movement caught her eye. Eli sat up and laughed, hugging her tight. "Can we press pause for a minute? I think I have a bite."

She glanced beyond him and saw that one of the fishing poles was indeed being dragged toward the lake. She leaped off of him and let him grab it, watching as he reeled it in.

"I hope whatever it is is big enough for dinner because all of a sudden I'm starved."

He motioned her over, and she put her arm around his waist as he continued to reel in the line. Just then the other line twitched, the pole it was attached to bent almost in half. "Can you get that?" he said. "I'm a little busy here."

"Gladly." The next several minutes were spent getting their catches closer to shore. They were two beautiful bass. More than enough for the both of them for dinner. But when he started to land his, she reached out a hand to stop him. "Eli, let's let them go."

He tilted his head and must have read something in her eyes because he nodded and waded in to pull the hook from first his fish and then repeated the process with hers, watching as they both swam away. "Here's to freedom."

Tears blurred her vision as she realized he'd understood exactly what she'd meant. "Yes. Here's to freedom. And to forevers."

With that, both poles were abandoned on the ground as they took up where they left off, both promising the other that today was the first of many days. And Georgia knew in her heart that it was true.

EPILOGUE

THE HOSPITAL'S YEARLY 5K run in Knicker Park was today. And both Eli and Georgia had signed up to be in it. But they didn't run. Instead, they walked hand in hand, talking about the future and what their hopes and dreams were.

Eli had taken her necklace in to have it repaired, and the butterfly charm was once again around her neck. And she'd told him that while it still meant freedom to her, that freedom no longer meant she had to be alone. He was her companion on this journey, and there was nowhere he would rather be.

She'd also bought him an engagement present. A narrow black braided wristband with a silver bead, also engraved with a butterfly. He loved it. Wore it whenever he was not doing surgery.

Edna had texted him from Florida saying that she was doing great and following her doctor's orders to take it easy. She was getting stronger every day. They'd already booked an Alaskan cruise for next summer, and she'd promised she and Artie would stop in to see them.

They'd attended Brandon's memorial service two weeks ago, and while it had been a time of sadness, Ted had asked Eli about the Big Brothers program after seeing a flyer on the wall of his office. His heart function was still doing well and the stents were doing their job, and he was looking to the future. He talked about seeing what Dutch Harbor had in the way of mentorship programs to try to help at-risk youths like Brandon. Eli had no doubt that Ted would do a great job and that it would also help fill the void left by the passing of his son.

The last couple of weeks had been filled with activity, both in their professional lives and in their private lives. Georgia had given up the lease on her studio apartment and had moved in with Eli. She said she wanted to get married as soon as possible, so their days were filled with lying in bed with brochures and making love. Her mom had flown up from Kodiak to help Georgia shop for wedding dresses. They'd found one the very first day they'd gone out shopping, and while his fiancée was happy with her choice, she told him he would have to wait until their wedding day to see it.

And that was okay with him. At least this time there was going to be a wedding day. And he knew that theirs would be for keeps. They'd met Steve and Julia at the cabin, and they'd celebrated their engagement with steaks cooked over the fire and a lot of laughter.

Eli was happier than he could ever imagine he'd be. Squeezing Georgia's hand, he let it go so that he could wrap an arm around her waist. "I think the finish line is just up ahead."

She smiled, pulling his head down for a kiss. "Do you think we're the last ones to arrive?"

"Does it matter?"

"No. It doesn't matter at all."

They got to the line that had been taped to indicate the end of the race and stood on it and kissed some more. The place was almost deserted, but they didn't care. What was someone else's finish line was their starting line. Their lives together were just taking off.

And who knew how high they would soar?

* * * * *

*Look out for the next story in the
Alaska Emergency Docs duet*
One-Night Baby with Her Best Friend
by Juliette Hyland

*And if you enjoyed this story,
check out these other great reads
from Tina Beckett*

ER Doc's Miracle Triplets
Tempting the Off-Limits Nurse
A Daddy for the Midwife's Twins?

All available now!